Cromwell's Boy

Cromwell's Boy

Erik Christian Haugaard

Houghton Mifflin Company Boston

Library of Congress Cataloging in Publication Data

Haugaard, Erik Christian.
  Cromwell's boy.

  Sequel to A messenger for Parliament.
  SUMMARY: A thirteen-year-old spy's wit and
horsemanship make him invaluable to the Cromwell
forces as they fight against King Charles.
  [1. Great Britain—History—Civil War,
1642-1649—Fiction] I. Title.
PZ7.H28Cr   [Fic]   78-14392
ISBN 0-395-27203-3

Printed in the United States of America

HC ISBN 0-395-27203-3
PB ISBN 0-395-54975-2

AGM 10 9 8 7 6 5 4 3 2 1

For my brothers, Niels and Dan

Contents

Cromwell's Boy

1

Boston, 1686

Summer is gone, the evenings are growing longer, and I have pulled my little boat on shore, for the waves in the bay have chilly fingers. Though autumn is a pleasant season with many a fair day, I have reached an age when it is difficult to be young if my feet are cold. Still, I have kept enough of a boy's heart to understand the secrets the wind whispers to me. Though the hand which grabs the tiller of my boat is bony and vein covered, the thrill of steering my vessel has not altogether left me. When age comes, your body plays traitor to your mind, and frailty conquers what is left of strength. But those who are able to love youth, even when it is passed, love it because its echo is still resounding in their souls.

Youth, a word to whisper, a time of promises all too rarely kept. Did I keep mine? Not all of them, I am sure, even though I made few. In my youth there was little time for dreams. Life challenged me early. The leisure to reflect was not my lot; tomorrow was ever knocking on the door of today with new demands. It made me resourceful and sharpened my wit, but the purpose of life must be more than just to survive. You must be able — at least for short moments — to hold your precious soul in your hands and to contemplate that gift with love and understanding.

Here in the colonies all the news has been unpleasant. Only those who deem that saying true that "misery loves company" have reason to rejoice. We lost our charter — our rights to be free men — and Rhode Island and New Hampshire have fared no better. Sir Edmund Andros rules more powerfully here than does James II in England. Andros is a name used to frighten children; unfortunately, it scares their parents as well. "Governor" is his title, but the word *despot* would better fit his character.

Last winter I told the story of a child: a leaf blown by the wind; how I by chance became a messenger for Parliament and was befriended by Oliver Cromwell. Oh, that name is still magic, and not only to me. It conjures up a world when you mention it. Not King, but Lord Protector of England was his title, and it would be difficult to name a more august one. Yet while he ruled, many an honest man prayed: "May the Lord protect me from Oliver Cromwell!"

Only fools or scoundrels will lay claim to tell the true story of their lives. The Lord may know the secrets of our hearts, but we seldom do. It is not only the blind that cannot see, nor the deaf that cannot hear. I shall not preach you a sermon upon the causes of that war which ravaged England and set brother against brother to leave a legacy of hatred. You must be satisfied with less: a tale for the chimney corner.

"Cromwell's boy," that is what I was called by the men of his regiment, so it is a fitting title for my story. But where should I begin? If I were to describe every moment of my life I would need an ocean of ink. The storyteller's art is one of selection; he picks up pebbles on the beach, most of which he throws away, keeping only those which have been worn into curious and strange shapes by the turbulent sea.

As we go through our lives, our titles change. The son becomes a father; the boy a merchant, a sea-captain, a farmer, or an alderman. Some of us advance and some do not. The promising young man can become the wastrel or even worse. To most of my neighbors in Boston, I am probably that "lonely old man, who sails a boat in summer and mutters to himself as he walks along the street."

But what was Cromwell's boy like? I cannot help smiling, for I see him clearly before me, galloping along the roads between Huntingdon, Cambridge, and Ely. He could ride! That was my talent when I was a youth. Once my legs were astride a horse, Oliver Cutter and that beast became one animal. It was this ability which made me of value to Colonel Cromwell. Orders and messages were continually being sent from one town to another. Fleetness was essential; and though I was only a child, too young by right to be on the rolls of the regiment, I rode one of its best horses.

I had another virtue which Oliver Cromwell and his fellow officers appreciated: I was by nature silent. A messenger may hear that which was not meant for his ears, and he can start rumors which could endanger the army. I was as solitary then as I am now. Oh, there were many reasons for this. I was an only child, brought up in poverty. My mother died when I was eleven, and I had ever before me the example of my father. He was one of those whose titles are ever diminishing till "drunkard" and "braggart" fitted him best. In my heart, I even begrudged him his rightful claim of being my parent. Through the first twelve years of my life, until the chances of war separated us, I had heard him boasting of the great deeds he either had done or would do: tissues of lies spoken to hide his failures. In my youth, my greatest fear was that I would grow up to be like him; therefore, I weighed my words before I spoke.

At thirteen I was not tall but could no longer be called small for my age. Although I was the same boy that I described last winter, I had changed: I was more sure of myself and possibly a little vain. During those months since I had come under Colonel Cromwell's protection, many a fair word had been spoken to and about me; and it is hard not to believe that which is pleasant.

My connection with the officers was a curious one, for it was said that I had Cromwell's ear. It is true that I was often in his presence; besides, I had been befriended by Bettie, the Colonel's favorite child, who was only a few months older than I. Some whispered that I was Oliver Cromwell's bastard son; an honor which I answered with a smile and so small a shake of the head that it could be mistaken for a nod.

On the 13th of May 1643, Cromwell won a battle at Grantham. It was almost a year since the King had raised his standard in Nottingham and turned England into a battlefield. The army of Parliament was still weak. Colonel Cromwell's troops were better disciplined than the rest; yet his regiment, too, was plagued by desertion, and he had renegades whipped. The Colonel's enemies said that the battle of Grantham had been merely a skirmish; for even then there were many who disliked Cromwell. But Parliament was in need of victories, and that battle made his name known to all.

In July, Colonel Cromwell took to the field again, moving north from Huntingdon to relieve the town of Gainsborough, which was besieged by the King's army. Along the way, he captured Burghley House. His men outnumbered the cavaliers by more than thirty to one, so it was no reflection on the courage of the defenders that they surrendered; yet this, too, bolstered Parliamentary spirits.

Here I shall start the story of Cromwell's boy. Outside my window it is raining and heavy clouds cover the sky. But if I close my eyes, I see the summer skies of England. There is the long train of troops and wagons on the road to Gainsborough; a little to the rear of the officers is a small speck: a boy riding a bay mare, the gentle winds of July playing with his locks. I shall tell you what happened to him, and should the truth at times lose its way in that crooked passage which runs from eye to mouth, judge me not too harshly.

2

The Battle of Gainsborough

"Oliver!" Colonel Cromwell called. I touched the flanks of my horse and rode quickly to his side.

"Go to the rear and see how the supply wagons are faring."

I turned my mare. To ride against an army on the march is as difficult as swimming against the current of a swift river. It took all my skill as a horseman and I received little thanks from those in whose way I got.

"Two of the wagons broke down. One was beyond re-repair," said the lieutenant in charge of the train of supplies. He looked harassed. His was not an enviable lot: If he did his work well he would receive no glory; but if the shaft of one of the wagons broke, he would be held responsible as if he had split it himself.

"I had the supplies reloaded onto a couple of carts," he grumbled.

I nodded and he looked away. I did not ask where the carts had come from. Somewhere behind us there was one farmer, if not more, who would now curse the army of Parliament.

As I rode away, I thought, "If anyone complains about the theft of a cart, the lieutenant will be blamed; and yet if the supplies had been lost he would have been in an even worse position." I was thankful I was only a messenger.

"That is well," Colonel Cromwell said when I reported to him that the supplies were following as quickly as could be expected. With a slight wave of his hand he indicated that I should fall back.

We were some twelve miles from Gainsborough, at a small village called North Scarle, when the troops of Lord Willoughby joined ours. Now it seemed to me that we were so many regiments of foot and horse that we could conquer all of England. It was a gay and splendid scene, and I thought that no life could be finer than that of a soldier.

It was my ignorance that made me believe our army was invincible. I saw soldiers where, in truth, there were only armed farmers, artisans, and runaway apprentices. Nor were they well armed. Many of the mounted men did not even carry pistols; and those who did, as often as not, had weapons with poorly made flintlocks that could not be depended upon to fire. Most of their swords were the work of a village blacksmith, and had neither strength nor sharp edges. As for their armor, only some of the men had breastplates or iron headpieces; more wore only caps, and there were those who did not even have a proper heavy leather coat.

As we neared the besieged town of Gainsborough, we encountered a small contingent of the King's dragoons. They were easily routed; but they made Colonel Cromwell wary, and he ordered the army to spread out in order to offer room for quick movement.

His caution proved wise. On approaching a hill that commanded the road over which our supplies would have to pass, we found that it was held by Royal forces. The more permanent proprietors of the heights were rabbits, and the holes they had burrowed were just perfect for breaking the leg of a horse.

The foot soldiers of Lord Willoughby, who were Lincolnshire men, were in the vanguard. They rushed up the hill to give battle, while we on horseback looked for a trail, free of rabbit holes, by which to gain the crest.

I should have stayed below, for I was unarmed, carrying only a dagger in my belt. What I did was against the Colonel's orders, for he had told me that in case of battle I was to retire to the wagons.

To ride with the rest up that hill was not bravery but foolishness; yet I did it. Was it that fever which comes to a soldier as he goes into battle that had overcome me? All I shall ever know for certain is that I followed the man in front of me, as a sheep follows its leader.

The men of Lincolnshire were in the center, with a regiment of horse on either side. We were well spread out. As we came near the top of the hill, the Royal forces charged. Now we had only the choice between fleeing and attacking.

The ground was not the best, for we would be fighting uphill. Yet none hesitated. With drawn swords and at a gallop, the opposing troops met each other.

There were but few shouts. It was bloody work: sword against sword, horse against horse.

"What brings you here, boy?" a giant of a man whom I knew by sight was shouting at me.

His words brought me to my senses. What, indeed, was I doing there, weaponless as I was? And I reined in my horse.

"Get back!" With a string of curses the soldier passed me, and I turned my mare.

Once free of the tumult, I stopped and looked back. The Royal troops were fleeing and our men were pursuing them.

But the battle was not over. The enemy held in reserve a regiment of horse and some troops of foot soldiers commanded by Colonel Cavendish.

Not far from me, next to a Royal soldier who would never ride again, lay a sword. I leapt from my horse and picked it up. I swung it in the air. It was light and finely made. Its edges were so sharp that had I been able to grow a beard, I could have shaved with it. It was a precious weapon, but it had not saved the life of the man who had owned it. I recalled a youngster whom I had been with at the Battle of Edgehill. He had longed for just such a sword, because he thought it the emblem of manhood.

I almost let the weapon fall to the ground, for it had occurred to me that this gift was of the devil, and once I called the sword mine, I should never be able to get rid of it again. Yet I kept it.

No sooner had I remounted, than the second part of the battle began. Colonel Cavendish advanced, routing what was left of the Lincolnshire troops. All around me they were falling back; and suddenly I was in the midst of the fighting.

Had Colonel Cromwell not succeeded in halting the Parliamentary cavalry, who were still pursuing the fleeing cavaliers, we might have duplicated the folly of Prince Rupert's men at Edgehill: of being more eager than wise. But unlike the Royal troops, our men responded to orders and returned to the field. Colonel Cavendish had to abandon his attack on the exhausted men of Lincolnshire and face about to defend himself.

All battles are a mass of confusion to those who take part in them. Most of the time you are fighting not to win but to survive, guarding your own little precious life.

I kept my sword ready to parry any blow aimed at me, rather than to strike myself. A young cavalier sought me out, probably because he believed I would be an easy conquest. His first attack I repulsed, my sword deflecting his.

He turned his horse and advanced towards me once more, his weapon lifted for what I feared would be my death blow. I held my sword out in front of me and dug my heels into the sides of my mare. Startled, the poor beast leapt forward and my sword pierced the chest of the cavalier!

He cried out, as his weapon dropped from his hand. Wildly he tried to grasp the blade of my sword, which was now red with his blood. His horse swerved and the cavalier fell from his saddle.

What breadth of time did all this take? How many ticks of the clock? Stupefied, I looked down at the young man, who with sightless eyes stared back at me.

I heard the calling of words of command nearby. It was Colonel Cromwell's voice. Around me the enemy were fleeing, their only thought now being to escape. Down the hill they went, with our troops chasing them, shouting as they swung their swords.

"Oliver!" The Colonel had seen me and I trotted dutifully towards him. He and some of his officers had reined in their horses and were contemplating the scene.

"What are you doing here?" the Colonel demanded sternly.

I did not answer but looked unhappily down at my sword.

His eyes followed mine. "You are pale," he said. "Are you wounded?"

"No, sir," I whispered and shook my head.

"Go to the rear and tell the lieutenant in charge of supplies that the road to Gainsborough is clear." Though his manner was still severe, there was a tone of kindness in his voice.

I was grateful to have once more a duty to perform. Carefully, remembering the rabbit holes, I started down the hill.

"You have killed a man," I thought, as I wiped my sword on the coat of my horse. "What did he look like?" I asked myself. I could not remember! And the tears ran down my cheek. Whether it was for the young cavalier or myself that I was crying I do not know.

3

An Orderly Retreat

A besieged city is much like an abandoned orphan. The garrison at Gainsborough had been cut off for so long that in despair they believed even Cambridge had fallen to the King. Their store of powder had been almost exhausted and all the other supplies that we brought were sorely needed. As our wagons entered the streets, there was much rejoicing.

We were asked a thousand questions, most of which we could not answer or did not wish to, for in truth, the cause of Parliament was not doing well. The tired troops of Gainsborough wanted to hear of victory not defeat, so we made much of our recent triumph. Nor was this unjust: the Royal forces had, after all, been totally vanquished, and Colonel Cavendish, the second son of the Earl of Devonshire, had been mortally wounded. But we were to pay dearly for our display of pride. Before the sun set, we were to learn the bitter lesson that Lincolnshire still belonged to King Charles.

"When will we take Newark?" one of the young men who was unloading the wagons asked me.

"When our Colonel sneezes, we shall teach the King to

14

say 'God bless you!' ... But all in good time," I answered, rather pleased with my own reply.

"I think it more likely that the King will wipe our noses, and bloody them as well," he grumbled.

"Boy!" someone called in a very commanding voice, and I looked around. It was the trooper who had cursed me at the beginning of the battle. He did not seem as formidable now as he had then, although he was an unusually big man. Prepared to receive the rough side of his tongue, I rode towards him.

"I beg your pardon for the words I spoke." He sounded more angry than conciliatory.

"But they were just!" I protested.

"I took the Name of Our Lord in vain. How can we win a war when we cannot even curb our tongues?" The soldier looked grimly down at his hands that lay folded on his saddle.

"Surely, in the heat of battle, a curse may slip from the lips of any man," I argued. Although Colonel Cromwell had issued a command that anyone heard cursing must pay a fine, it was a rule not much obeyed as yet.

"Did not St. Matthew say in his Gospel: 'Swear not at all, and not by heaven for that is God's throne'?" The soldier shook his head.

"But it is also said that God is merciful," I muttered.

"If we be the saints who will cleanse England, then surely our tongues should only praise the Lord!"

This was the first time that I heard anyone refer to himself as a saint, though later it became common among those who believed that the war was a crusade of the righteous.

"But what were you doing there?" he demanded with that edge of disgust that seemed natural to his voice. "You could have caused the death of some soldier of Christ!"

"I am Colonel Cromwell's messenger," I said proudly.

"And had he sent you into battle without a sword or a pistol? Your mare could have been killed, and she is a fine beast!"

I shrugged my shoulders; I could not argue with the trooper for I knew that he was right. "No," I mumbled. "I should not have been there."

"You obey your elders, lad, and do not go where you are not wanted." With his heels, the giant touched the flanks of his horse and rode on.

Suddenly drums were beating for assembly. What could have happened? Everyone rushed towards the sound.

Royal dragoons had been sighted to the north of the town. One regiment of horse and four hundred Lincolnshire foot soldiers, under Major Whalley, were to advance and intercept them.

"Oliver!" Major Whalley called out, "I might have need of a messenger. Stay close to me." He grinned. "Now that you are a swordsman as well, you can protect me."

I blushed as I fell in behind the Major. I had picked up a sheath for my sword; it was a rough leather covering which ill-fitted the weapon. I had found it among the booty that is collected after every battle. I had also spied there a sheath that might have belonged to my sword. It had silver fittings. But I had chosen the clumsy leather one. This I had done, not to hide the sword from the envious eyes of others — though that may have been wise — but to conceal it from myself. I was not yet a veteran and that harvest which takes place after a battle, I still considered stealing.

The Royal dragoons fled as soon as they saw us; and we in high spirits pursued them. When they suddenly disappeared behind a small hill, we galloped eagerly up the slope. But as we approached the crest of the hill, without any orders being given, as one man, we all reined in our horses. Like a long line of statues, we sat gazing at the sight below us.

Advancing towards Gainsborough, like a great river in flood, was the whole army of the Marquis of Newcastle! I counted fifty colors of foot soldiers and many more regiments of horse than we could muster. The Royal dragoons had merely been a party of scouts, who no doubt were already reporting what they had seen to their superiors.

"We are outnumbered ten — if not twenty — to one!" I thought. Yet I felt no fear as I looked at the spectacle below me, but admired it as I might have a beautiful sunset.

"Oliver." Major Whalley's voice was calm. He was smiling as if he, too, were moved by the sight of that vast army such a short distance away. "Ride as fast as your horse can carry you. Tell the Colonel what you have seen." He paused. "I shall try to shield the foot soldiers until they are safely inside the town. Now hurry! Begone!"

I did not dare to tell him my thoughts, which were that Gainsborough would not hold against a horde like this, nor would they need trumpets to make the walls fall.

I dug my heels into the flanks of my horse and galloped away.

I passed the men of Lincolnshire, who had not as yet reached the top of the hill, and therefore knew nothing of what we had seen. An officer called out to me, but I did not stop. Never have I ridden faster. The wind blew past my ears as though it were storming.

Colonel Cromwell was busy inspecting the defenses of the town and had not yet dismounted. How I delivered the message, I cannot remember. The words came tumbling out, one on top of the other. But I do recall the expression on the Colonel's face.

He watched me carefully as he listened intently to what I was saying. He did not frown, but a few wrinkles appeared in his forehead. When I finished, he looked around him, and I think his glance took in once more the defenses of Gainsborough.

"Ten to one," he whispered and shook his head. For a moment he sat silent and impassive on his horse. I do not know, but I think he might have been praying. Then he called several officers to him and issued commands rapidly:

All the troops of horse were to assemble outside the city; and as soon as the men of Lincolnshire, who were with Major Whalley, had entered, the gates of Gainsborough were to be closed.

The opposite of advance is not flight but retreat; and, from what I have seen of war, it is by far the most difficult maneuver. Had Colonel Cromwell stayed in Gainsborough, then he and the best regiments of horse in the entire Parliamentary army would have been taken prisoner when Gainsborough fell to the Marquis of Newcastle. The town was a trap for mounted soldiers. Inside its walls they were of no greater worth than foot soldiers. Colonel Cromwell never hesitated to abandon what he considered lost.

Most of the men had had their fill of fighting. They were tired and so were their horses. A soldier's heart is like the pendulum of a clock, forever swinging between great expectations and hopeless despair. One moment life smiles upon him and the next death grins and beckons him. A wrong word, a wrong movement by those in command, and all discipline is lost and retreat becomes defeat.

Back along the same road we had taken that morning, we went; but now the men were silent and their faces grim. The Colonel waited until Major Whalley arrived with the Lincolnshire foot soldiers; several regiments of Royal dragoons were at their heels. When the Lincolnshire men entered Gainsborough, the gates of the luckless town were closed behind them.

Colonel Cromwell had sent me ahead with the first regiment to leave. All of us kept glancing back over our shoulders, expecting at any moment to see our enemy.

An ensign came galloping up from the rear. When he reached us, he slowed down to a trot and shouted as loudly as he could: "Turn whenever we are attacked! Let no man see your back but only your sword! Each man guards the man beside him; and let none allow his horse to gallop. These are the Colonel's orders." The ensign grinned. "Should any of you be in a hurry to get back to a sick mother, you must ask Colonel Cromwell for permission first!"

What his last sentence lacked in wit, it made up for by being timely. As long as the officers can joke, the men will keep up their spirits. Still, one man riding not far from me did grumble loudly that his horse was too weary to carry him.

"Then get off and put the saddle on your own back and give the poor beast a ride," the ensign, who had heard the remark, shouted.

"Do!" screamed one of his comrades. "Methinks I would like to see a horse mounted on an ass." This comment caused much laughter and coarser jokes followed, each soldier trying to still the fear in his own heart by laughing louder than the man next to him.

But we were allowed to retreat unscathed and lost not one man. Each time we were attacked, counterattacks were made. Slowly, until night came, we fought and retreated, repeating again and again the same maneuver. The Royal forces, though far greater than ours, never charged us head on.

When they finally turned and left us in peace, each man felt that he had taken part not in a defeat but in some kind of glorious victory.

4
In Ely

"Have you come to take my father away again?" Bettie Cromwell looked at me very seriously.

"I brought letters from Major Whalley. I know not what is in them." I was seated at the table in the kitchen of the Colonel's home. It was several weeks after the Royal forces had captured Gainsborough.

"I wish my father would stay right here in Ely and never go anywhere else!" The girl frowned. "Why couldn't Cousin Edward come here himself?"

I shrugged my shoulders. Bettie was always asking me questions that I could not possibly know the answers to. "Major Whalley has much to look after in Huntingdon," I finally replied.

"Captain Ireton has been here, but I like Cousin Edward better."

I nodded. I, too, preferred Major Whalley to Captain Ireton, who wore an expression on his face as if doomsday were tomorrow. "The Colonel thinks much of the Captain." I looked at Bettie; the statement had been half a question.

"My father says that God has given the Captain great gifts." Her tone made me suspect that for once Bettie Cromwell did not agree with her father. The girl sensed that I had been aware of her disloyalty and quickly added, "I do think that Captain Ireton is very clever."

"No one thinks the Captain a fool, but the men prefer Major Whalley."

"I am glad they like Cousin Edward." Bettie paused. "I like him much, too." Then she blushed.

Her embarrassment was contagious and we both became silent. "She loves her cousin," I thought, "but she is still a child and loves him as Master Powers's daughter, Faith, in Oxford loved me." My reasoning pleased me, for it made me feel older than Bettie, though in truth, she was born a few months earlier than I.

"My father told me that you killed a man at a battle near Gainsborough." The girl looked at me expectantly and I thought she wanted me to deny it.

"Aye," I answered and frowned. The night before I had dreamed of the fighting; but in my dream I had been the one who had died. I had awakened covered with sweat as if I had had a fever. "I had but little choice," I mumbled.

"You were not afraid?"

I looked up at Bettie. I had been wrong; she was proud of me.

"Not then. I was not afraid then, for everything happens

so quickly during a battle." As I answered I realized that fear fed on time and had I had even a few minutes to reflect before I attacked my opponent, I might not be alive now.

"I wish the war were over. Every time my father goes away I fear that he will never come back," Bettie whispered and bowed her head, "I pray for him . . . But then I think that God might not hear me because there are so many prayers being said."

"He will hear you," I insisted and to my surprise my voice sounded more convincing than I felt.

"But someone prayed for the man you killed," Bettie argued.

"Aye, but none prayed for me," I said with bitterness, for I should have liked to have a sister who could pray to God that I would return.

"But . . . but I did . . ." Bettie blushed again.

"Thank you," I mumbled and my cheeks too were flushed; and then, though I did not believe it to be true, I said, "The war will soon be over."

"Bettie!" someone called.

Although neither of us had noticed it, Bridget had entered the kitchen. "Our mother wants you in the linen room," Bridget said to her sister. Then, turning to me, she announced, "Colonel Cromwell asked me to tell you that he wishes to see you."

It was not lost on me that Bridget Cromwell had not said "Father" but referred instead to his rank. Of all of Cromwell's children, she was the only one whom I had good reason to believe disliked me. I think she considered high spirit an affront to God, and laughter almost a mortal sin. She always dressed in somber colors and was rather like a small dark cloud which casts a large shadow. As I passed her, I wondered if she had ever prayed for anyone's safe return.

Colonel Cromwell was writing when I entered the room; and although he did not even look up, I was aware that something had annoyed him.

"This," he finally said, as he finished, "is a note for Major Whalley." Carefully, he sprayed a bit of sand over the letter, then shook the paper above a little box that stood next to his table. Then, very much to my surprise, he asked, "You know London, do you not, Oliver?"

"Not as well as if I had been born there," I answered.

"But if I remember correctly, you told me that you had sold news-sheets on the streets of London."

"I did, sir," I replied more loudly than I had intended. "Master Waldon's *Mercurius,* it was called."

"You are young to be sent so far away, but you will have an escort. And you have served me well. There are two virtues one might ask of a messenger, first that he is not a fool ... If you lose your way, be careful of whom you ask directions ... Second, one can expect that a messenger's throat is not perpetually dry, for after visiting too many ale houses, he might not be able to see the difference between me and ..." he paused and smiled bitterly, "handsome Prince Rupert."

"Before I ask anyone the way, I shall first demand to know

whom they serve," I said. I knew that the Colonel was referring to an incident which had happened only recently near the town of Boston in Lincolnshire, where a messenger from Parliament had been caught because he had asked directions from a group of Royal dragoons.

"This letter is for my cousin Oliver St. John, whom you will find in Lincoln's Inn," Colonel Cromwell said, handing it to me. "And this," he held out the one he had just written, "is for Major Whalley."

As I put the letters away in the pouch which I carried in my belt, I noticed that he had not bothered to seal the one to the Major; and this pleased me for it showed how much the Colonel trusted me.

"Have they fed you?" he asked.

"Yes, sir," I answered. "I have been well taken care of."

"You may sleep the night in Huntingdon, but be on your way by morning. Major Whalley will give you further instructions and supply the money for your keep. He will also choose the men to accompany you."

"If you wish me to hasten, I could start tonight," I suggested, although it would be the first time that I had ridden through the darkness.

"The morning will do." The Colonel leaned back in his chair and looked at me. "Robert's jerkin fits you well."

"Yes, sir," I mumbled. I knew how difficult it was for Colonel Cromwell even to pronounce the name of his dead first-born son. "I am very proud of it," I said, while I fingered the leather jerkin nervously.

"If you have need of more clothes, there must be some too small for the other boys."

"Thank you," I muttered, hardly loud enough to be heard.

"Be not shy to ask. I count you one of us." The Colonel smiled. "You can ask one of my daughters; they will gladly see to you. I have use for as many Olivers as I can get; and if the Lord has sent me one a little young, methinks his spirit makes up for his age and size."

Colonel Cromwell was always kind to his family and those whom he deemed his friends; nevertheless, I was too embarrassed to answer.

He sensed my discomfort and walked with me to the door. "God speed, my boy," he said. "And may you bring back good news."

5
Major Whalley

By late afternoon I was in Huntingdon and had delivered Colonel Cromwell's letter to Major Whalley. His servant told me to return as soon as I had seen to my horse and had my supper.

I wiped down my mare, for she was sweaty from the ride, and then let her out to graze. She was a four-year-old, brown with a white star on her forehead. I watched her as she daintily sniffed the grass before she ate it. She was a fine animal.

Shortly after our return from Gainsborough, I had entered into an agreement with a widow: For a small sum, I rented a room in her attic and she cooked my breakfast and supper. She was to be paid by the week, and I owed her for two. She had not complained, though I knew she had little to spare.

When I returned to my lodging, carrying my saddle and bridle, I told her that I had eaten well in Ely and had no need for supper. But she would hear none of this and gave me soup and bread and cheese. She was the kind of woman who seemed to take pleasure in seeing her guests eat. There were several other soldiers living there, and each spoonful any of us ate she considered a compliment to her cooking.

I had to wait to see the Major; and by the time I was called in, the sun had set. He was sitting by a table on which a single candle was burning. His brow was furrowed; he was writing a letter. He looked up at me, and with a wave of his hand, he indicated a chair; then bent his head over his work again.

I sat and watched him. The letter must have been a difficult one, for he paused often and once he scratched his nose with the end of the goose feather, which almost made me laugh. I felt more at ease with the Major than with any of the other officers, for though he could be demanding, he was never slow to give praise if you deserved it. He carried his rank well and had the ability to be friendly to those who served under him without losing their esteem. I think this virtue most important in those who are in command; and there were many of the other officers who lacked it.

When he had finished his letter, he read it through once and then put it down next to the candle and sighed. I thought he had completely forgotten me, when suddenly he asked, "Oliver, what say the men about the Covenant? . . . The Solemn League and Covenant."

The question surprised me, for he must have known as well as I did that the Covenant with the Scots, which we all would have to sign, was not popular with the men. It had been part of a bargain, which — if kept — would make England Presbyterian.

"Some say that the difference between a presbyter and a bishop is that the first wears the devil's horns and the other his tail," I answered and grinned.

The Major smiled grimly. "We are in need of the Scots — but more of their arms than their religion. They are to supply an army of twenty-one thousand men and for that we are to agree to reform our church to their liking."

Because my father had swallowed the Bible and spat bits of it out in my face ever since I could distinguish day from night, I had no fondness for discussing religion.

"If the Irish, who are Catholic, will fight for the King, I suppose we need the Presbyterians of Scotland to balance the scale." These words were not my own, but borrowed from a soldier I much respected.

"For every Irishman the King brings across the sea, two Englishmen will run to our banner." The Major shook his head. "The Irish cannon is a faulty piece, and it will blow up when it is fired."

This was true, for every time it was rumored that the Irish had landed, the cause of Parliament gained recruits. "But, sir," I argued hesitantly. "Will not some of our men leave, if they have to fight side by side with the Scots?" I knew that many of those who called themselves Independents would revolt for sure if they had to take orders from presbyters.

"We shall not mix them in the regiments . . . But they will send us preachers." Major Whalley grimaced and added, "As if we were heathens."

"There will be those among us who will enjoy the arguments," I said shyly, thinking of the "saint" I had met at Gainsborough. He would be a nut that a Presbyterian nut-cracker would not easily break.

"Sparks will fly between them and the Anabaptists, you can be sure of that, Oliver." This prospect amused the Major enough to make him laugh. "But sign we must. We are not like Gideon who can send away his men and still win battles."

"Will the Colonel sign the Covenant?" I asked, for I knew that Colonel Cromwell considered himself to be an Independent and believed that godliness was more important than church attendance. He had even defended the Anabaptists, whom the Presbyterians hated.

"Cromwell will be the last to sign it, of that you can be sure." Major Whalley glanced down at the letter lying in front of him. "And I know one who will never sign it." Then he looked up at me. "We have been most satisfied with you, Oliver. Sending you to London is a mark of great trust. But I have confidence that your tongue will never wag what your ears have heard."

"I shall be dumb as if I were deaf," I said.

Major Whalley laughed. "I do believe you. You are carrying a letter from Colonel Cromwell to our cousin, Oliver St. John; do you know how important it is?"

I shook my head, uncertain whether I should answer yes or no.

"If you are caught, destroy it first, if you have time. We have asked our cousin to plead for us with Parliament for money to pay the troops. I have no wish for the King to know of our condition — though I think he is as short of silver as we are."

Major Whalley paused, and then, pointing to the letter he had just finished, he said, "I have another letter which I wish you to deliver in London . . . It is a personal one." For a moment, I thought that it was a love letter which the Major wanted me to carry, for he blushed. "It is to Master John Selden, who lives at White Friars, in the house of the Duchess of Kent."

"Shall I await a reply?" I asked wondering who this man might be, who caused Major Whalley such concern.

"If he thinks me worthy of it, I shall be pleased." The Major looked away, as if he preferred seeing no one while he spoke. "There is no man in England wiser than he is . . . Nor, I think, more just . . . I wish he were more whole-heartedly on our side. He is for Parliament, I know. But not at any cost. The star that guides him is like that bright stead-fast one you see as soon as the sun sets." Major Whalley rubbed his forehead. "I wish ours to shine as clearly . . . A Solemn League and Covenant." He shook his head, looked up at me and smiled. "If you see him, Oliver, mark in your mind his features, so that you can tell your grandchildren what John Selden looked like."

"I shall, sir," I declared, and the Major laughed.

"You see why your tongue must be tied. If you told of our doubts, half the army would desert us. You shall leave in the morning. Now go and find Sergeant Hampton and tell him to come here."

"Yes, sir." I bowed and turned to go, but at the door I tarried a moment and said, "I shall do my best, sir."

"So shall we all, Oliver. So shall we all. May God not demand more of us."

As I closed the door behind me, I saw that the Major had risen and was standing at the window, deep in thought.

6
To London

The clatter of horses' hoofs is pleasant music to those who love to ride. I turned to glance at the two soldiers detailed to be my escort; they sat well in their saddles. "All who see me will think that I am the son of a lord," I thought proudly, and looked around me as I had seen Prince Rupert do when he rode through the streets of Oxford. But there was no one to admire me except the cows in the fields, and they cared for nothing but the grass which grew beneath their feet.

The road we had taken would lead us past my home, that poor cottage which my father and I had abandoned to go "a-soldiering," as he had called it. How many times during the last month had I been within a few miles of it; and yet I had not visited it, nor had I gone to see the blacksmith and his wife, though I owed them a debt of gratitude that I should never be able to repay.

I was a messenger for Colonel Cromwell. I rode a good horse and carried a sword at my side. Did I fear that once I stepped inside the damp walls of that hut in which I had been born, all I had achieved would vanish as if by magic, and I would be again the beggar boy to whom the generous gave a farthing and the rest of humanity their contempt?

As we drew nearer to that place which, when I was a small child, had been all the world to me, I recognized every bend of the road as it twisted and turned. I saw the gable of the smithy, shaded by the big apple tree that grew in the garden. Many of its fruits had ended up in my stomach. I smiled, recollecting how I had climbed among those branches; to my surprise, though large, it was not as huge as I remembered it.

When we passed the forge, I heard the sound of the hammer and caught a glimpse of the blacksmith through the open door. "He would be pleased to see me," I thought, "and amazed." I pulled on the reins, but then let them loose again. "No, I have been sent to London on errands of importance. It would not do to tarry."

But only a moment later, when I came to the cottage, I did rein in my horse. No one but the birds of the fields occupied it now. The thatch on the roof was filled with holes. The untrod path to the door was overgrown. Everything looked desolate; and yet while my mother lived it had been filled with warmth. Without hesitating, I jumped down from my horse and handed the reins to one of my companions.

"I'll be back in a few minutes," I said, not wishing to explain.

Like the blacksmith's apple tree, the cottage had shrunk. I put my shoulder to the door and forced it open. A damp, decaying smell met me, like the vapors from a tomb. The fireplace was filled with twigs dropped by the jackdaws who had built their nest in the chimney. Our one window had been taken out, leaving a gaping hole in the wall. The white-wash had peeled away. But the ladderlike stairs that led to the loft were still there; and so was the rope that my father had swung from one of the rafters, through the opening in the ceiling, to make it easier to climb the steps. I touched the rope, which, through the years, had been worn smooth.

The loft was as bare as the room below; through a hole in the roof, I found myself looking at the sky. "Mother," I whispered, but she was no longer there. Not enough had been left even for a ghost.

As I closed the door of the cottage, I thought, "Now you will never return."

I looked down at the big stone before the entrance. With my boot, I pushed the long grass aside, so I could see the edge which my father had worn away by sharpening his tools. Where was he now? Was he still a scrivener, or had his wagging tongue and endless thirst made him a vagabond again? I had seen him last on the streets of Worcester, look-ing for someone — anyone! — to whom he might tell the news that he had learned from the lieutenant for whom he wrote and kept accounts.

"My father is a fool and a drunkard." I mumbled out loud the words that I had so often thought, and I was sur-prised at how little bitterness there was in them. "He can-not help it," I silently remarked.

As I swung myself into the saddle, I decided that when I returned from London I would visit the blacksmith. His wife had brought me into the world; and it was she who had nursed my mother and closed her eyes when she died. "I must bring her a gift," I thought, and I felt as virtuous as though I had already given it to her.

There is not much to tell about my ride to London. Major Whalley had chosen my companions wisely. They were sober young men who would keep me from trouble rather than lead me into it. Their tongues were not cut for talking. They did not store up words as misers do gold; they were mute because they found no pleasure in conversation. I do not think they envied me my post, but were thankful that they had been saved the embarrassment of having to deliver messages. They were big, strapping men; yet shy like young maidens.

We lodged one night at an inn, and on the second evening of our travel, just as darkness fell, we reached the city. We were to stay at the home of a family from Cambridgeshire. They were humble, country people; and my companions were visibly relieved when they realized that they were among their own kind instead of strangers.

It was too late for me to attend to my errands, for the streets of London are not safe once night lends its cloak to villains and robbers. We were given a good supper and good ale to wash it down with. I had but one pot of it, while my comrades became merry and ventured to string more than two words together. Their inspiration they drew not alone from the drink, but also from the two young daughters of the house. The girls giggled and blushed in turns, and dug their elbows into each other's sides, which caused more laughter and more blushing.

The father had a stern face and admonished his daughters several times for their levity. But their mother smiled and asked the young men a thousand questions. She wanted to know the size of the farms they came from, and whether the land was rented or freehold. She asked them not only how many brothers and sisters they had, but whether they were younger or older than the soldiers themselves. The young men answered readily enough. Either they were unaware of her designs or they did not disapprove of them. There were moments when I feared that she might include me in her matchmaking; but happily she deemed me too young. When I admitted that I was tired, I was quickly led to a tiny room in the attic.

I was thankful to be alone. I have always been solitary. I had neither brothers nor sisters; and only my father's cronies came to our little cottage. Until we went "a-soldiering" I had never known another child.

As I undressed, I recalled the first time I had been in London. "I was nothing but a pitiful waif then," I thought. But when I blew out the candle, the darkness that blotted out the world took some of my grandeur with it.

"And now?" I asked myself, "What am I now?"

I was still a boy and I longed for a friend my own age. "Jack," I whispered, as I drew my legs up and hugged my knees. He was the only friend I had ever had. Here in London we had sold Master Waldon's news-sheet, *Mercurius*. Together we had hawked from one ale house to the next, looking for customers. I grinned, remembering some of our adventures.

"Ow!" I had been bitten by a bedbug or a flea. I had forgotten to search the bedclothes before snuffing out the candle.

Where was Jack now? Probably in Oxford with his parents. His father was a vicar. I lay there stiffly, expecting to be bitten again.

Jack and I had been together in Oxford, too. We had stayed at an inn called "The Unicorn." The owner, Master Powers, had had a daughter; I closed my eyes in order to see her. "Faith," I murmured. Only yesterday Bettie Cromwell had reminded me of Faith because of the way she had talked about Major Whalley. Faith had said that she wanted to marry me, but she was only a child and little girls like to play getting married. Bettie and Faith lingered together in my mind until I could no longer tell them apart, and when they, like past and present, became one I fell asleep.

7

A Dinner Party

___

To someone like me, who has been brought up in the country, where everyone knows everyone else and the word "stranger" is no compliment, the city is both attractive and frightening. How do all these people live? What do they do? What is their work? In the country, everyone has his own particular position, like the wheels in a clock; and the great weight that makes all of them go around is the lord in his hall. But who was the lord of London? Who ruled this great multitude of men, women, and children?

As you walk along the streets you cannot help feeling a sense of freedom. The passers-by do not see you nor does every house have eyes that watch you. "Are they not lonely?" I asked myself, but then it occurred to me that in the country and the villages you could be lonely too; and in some ways your loneliness could be harder to bear because you suffered it among people whom you knew.

My first errand was quickly accomplished. I found Lincoln's Inn with little difficulty and the rooms of Oliver St. John with even less. He was not at home, but his servant said that he would put the letter into his hands as soon as he arrived. I thanked him and remarked that I would wait upon Oliver St. John the following morning, as he might have some word which he wished me to take back to my own master.

Such a situation would have flustered me only a few months ago, but now I was so used to it that I gave it little thought. I had realized that what was important in speaking with both masters and servants was to state clearly and frankly the reason why one had come. If you hesitate, stammer, whisper, or appear shy and embarrassed, the master will think you are a fool and the servant will deem you an impostor who has come to beg. Yet you must not appear haughty, especially to servants, for they are quick to evaluate your position in relationship to their own; and they like familiarity in those they consider beneath them even less than their masters do. As I was about to leave Oliver St. John's rooms in Lincoln's Inn, I received a slight bow from his servant, a middle-aged man, which I returned with the same civility.

White Friars was not far away, and I hastened to deliver my second letter. The house of the Duchess of Kent was an old abbey, where the white friars had lived and prayed in those times when all of England was Catholic and the pope ruled. The house was very grand and there were many servants about. Seeing one whom I judged from his dress might be of some importance, I asked him where I might find Master John Selden, as I had a letter for him.

Major Whalley had not told me what position John Selden

held in this household, but the deep respect with which the servant spoke of him convinced me that he was none other than the master, himself.

I waited in the entrance hall, on the walls of which hung many paintings. I had good time to study them, for more than an hour passed before anyone noticed me again.

An elderly servant, whom I guessed to be the lord of all the lesser ones, came to fetch me. He was — in his own eyes, at least — a very great man; and he did not waste his breath on me but merely beckoned to let me know that I should follow him.

We passed through several splendid rooms. In one of them I saw chairs with such thin legs that I was sure they would break if anyone sat down on them. Finally, we came to a large portal, the panels of which were carved with very strange figures. The servant threw open the door and, again by the use of his hand, indicated that I should enter.

I do not know what I had expected, but certainly not what I found: ten gentlemen, seated at a table, busily eating dinner. I bowed to the man at the head of the table and waited for his nod to announce my errand.

He held out his hand for the letter, and when I had given it to him he looked at it with curiosity; but then he put it down on the table beside his plate and turned his attention to me. He was a tall, thin man with long hair. He had a curved, sharp nose that was a little crooked, and his lips were full. But what you noticed most were his large, bluish-gray eyes.

"You come from Cambridgeshire. How fares Colonel Cromwell?" he asked.

"He is well, sir," I said, casting a sidelong glance at the men at the table, who were all looking at me.

"And the cause of Parliament? I understand he was sorely beaten at Gainsborough."

"He was not, sir; unless retreating without the loss of a single man, when your foe has ten times your strength, can be called being beaten. If that is so, then we were," I replied hotly. But then, feeling ashamed at my display of temper, I added, "We met the whole army of the Marquis of New-castle."

"We!" Master Selden smiled and turned to his friends. "Sirs, we are in the company of a veteran!"

The men laughed, and I could feel my cheeks burning. Master Selden seeing my plight must have felt sorry for me because he stilled the merriment by speaking to me very seriously, "I am glad that I was wrongfully informed. I hope that the rumors from the south prove as untrue. Was this your first battle, young man?"

I intended to lie and say, yes; but a "no" escaped me. "I was also at Edgehill," I explained.

This time I expected their laughter, but only a few of the men smiled; most of them looked at me with interest.

"At Edgehill, too? Are you not a little young to be so fervent a servant of Mars?"

Luckily, I had heard this particular phrase before and I

knew what it meant. "I carried no weapon then, sir. It was almost by mistake that I was there."

"What regiment were you in?" one of the gentlemen asked in such a manner that it was clear he was no stranger to Edgehill.

"I was on the left flank, sir," I replied, looking straight at him.

He smiled and winked. "Then you caught it hot enough. I was on the right myself."

A fat elderly man now spoke to me, as if he were addressing a large audience, and I thought he might be a clergyman. "And was that what gave you a taste for fighting?" he said.

"I have little taste for it, sir. Some think it a good meal and come back for more to satisfy their pleasure, but not I."

Master Selden laughed and some of his friends joined him. "That barb was meant for you, sir," he said, lifting his glass towards the old man.

I looked down at the floor. Finally, when I heard the gentlemen begin to speak among each other again, as if I weren't there, I took a few steps towards Master Selden and said quietly, "I know that Major Whalley would like an answer to your letter, for he told me that you were the wisest man in England. If you wish, I could come on the morrow for your reply."

For a moment I thought that Master Selden had not heard me, but then he turned and said very thoughtfully, "Your major was mistaken. I think there is many a man wiser than

I in England. Otherwise, God help us! . . . Come tomorrow at ten, I shall have attended to a letter for you to deliver to Major Whalley."

Master Selden raised his hand to call a servant, but then thought better of it and rose himself. With a smile on his lips, he led me to the door and opened it for me. As I passed by him, he put his hand on my shoulder and held it there. "You did well, boy," he whispered.

As I was about to leave White Friars, I heard someone clear his throat behind me. I turned; there was the old servant who had silently brought me to Master Selden. He handed me a sovereign and almost bowed. "Remember tomorrow at ten," he said solemnly.

8

I Meet Old Friends

I had now done both of my errands and had the rest of the day before me in which to indulge my own pleasure. The strange interview with Master John Selden was still uppermost in my mind. I did not doubt that I had been allowed in while he was dining in order to offer amusement to his guests. This I did not resent, because I believed that I had acquitted myself well and had a golden coin to prove it.

As I walked along the streets I felt that the world was not so evil a place as I had heard it described from the pulpit.

I wanted to see the house where I had stayed the first time I was in London. I wondered whether Master Waldon would recognize me. He had fed Jack and me and let us sleep on the floor of the room where he kept his printing press, in return for which we had sold his news-sheet. I remembered how frightened I had been of his mad daughter, Antonia. "I was only a child then," I thought and smiled to myself. It is always pleasurable to think of one's improvements, and I am afraid that mine had gone to my head and made me conceited.

The house looked abandoned. The front door had been damaged, and a board nailed across it, so that it could no longer be opened. The windows had been smashed and clumsily shielded in the same manner.

I knew there was a door in the garden wall, and although I expected to find it locked, I walked down the alley alongside the house, which led to it. To my surprise, it was not even closed.

The garden had never been tidy, but now it was a wilderness, and I could see that it had not been dug that spring.

As I lifted the latch to the back door, I put my shoulder to it; but I need not have. The door swung back almost of its own accord. Everything was filthy and from the ceilings hung great cobwebs.

But was it deserted? Though there was no fire in the kitchen, I felt that someone lived there still. Room after room looked as if a battle had taken place in it. Broken furniture littered the floors. The printing press had been damaged beyond repair, as though a blacksmith had smashed it with his heaviest hammer. I was standing staring at it, when I heard a slight noise behind me.

Someone had entered the room. It was Master Waldon, but so changed that I could hardly recognize him. His uncombed hair was totally white. His face was ingrained with dirt, like that of a vagabond who no longer lived in a house but slept in an alley like a dog. His clothes were rags. In his hand he held a stick on which he leaned heavily.

"Mr. Waldon, it is me, Oliver," I said. But the man stared

at me vacantly, and I thought he might be deaf as well, so I repeated my name a little louder and added, "What has happened here?"

"The wrath of God has fallen upon me and I am cursed like Job," the old man muttered, looking at his wrecked machine, of which I can remember his being so proud.

"This looks more like the wrath of men," I said. "Why was your printing press spoiled?" With my foot I stirred the debris.

"They were but God's instruments, like the birch that flogs the disobedient child. I paid no heed to my daughter, and she let the Antichrist rule in her heart! For this the Lord punished me. Pride was in my heart and I saw not the duty which was near me." Suddenly Master Waldon laughed. "Have you come to take me to the Tower?" he asked.

"No, sir. I am Oliver who stayed with you last winter. You remember my friend Jack . . ." I wished that I had never entered the house. I had heard that in London mobs had broken into the homes of Catholics; and now I recalled how I had seen them plundered and robbed during the sacking of Worcester. Poor Master Waldon's daughter had been Catholic; and her father, a supporter of Parliament, had paid for it with his ruin.

"Oliver . . . Oliver," he repeated my name, though I do not think he remembered me. "The Lord is jealous and he tolerates not that we worship idols. They took her life away most cruelly."

For a moment I thought he might mourn his daughter and condemn her murderers, but I was mistaken. The old man folded his hands in prayer. "Blessed be the Lord who scourgeth me, for he knows my sinful heart."

Poor Antonia had not had the wits of a clever child, although she was a full-grown woman. Her eyes had sometimes looked as frightened as those of a trapped animal. I turned to go away. The old man revolted me; even in his madness he thought only of himself.

"Sir . . . sir," eagerly Master Waldon called me back. "Have you not got a penny for a poor man?" He held out his hands. His fingernails were as long as claws.

I had left most of my money with the good man with whom I stayed; but besides my sovereign I had a shilling. I thrust it at him and quickly left the house; I did not want to hear his thanks. Yet once I was in the street again, I turned to look back. Suddenly I recalled that Master Waldon had kept a piece of Lord Strafford's shirt in a tiny leather pouch around his own neck. It was blood-stained because it had been worn on the day that poor man's head had rolled from the executioner's block. Master Waldon had paid well for it, as it was supposed to protect his health. "That charm had no power," I thought.

This should have been adventure enough for one day; but there was more in store for me, and I was to meet yet another old friend before the sun set.

I dined on a meat pie in an ale house; and it was as good and as filling a pie as I have ever put in my mouth.

How long I wandered through the streets I don't know, for there was so much that a boy from the country would stare at wide-eyed. At a small square, a tooth-puller had placed his chair. He had a little boy who beat a drum to attract customers. There was soon a crowd to watch the spectacle, and much joking and laughing when a poor victim with pale cheeks and trembling limbs sat down. One old man laughed so hard, each time the patient screamed, that I feared he might drop dead from merriment. He himself had not a tooth in his mouth, so I suppose he had no reason to be scared of the tooth-puller's tongs.

Being inland born I was drawn to water, and I walked down a narrow alley to see the river, that broad road which brings wares to London from all over the world.

The sun was about to set, and I decided that I ought to return to my lodgings, so for the last time I picked up a stone, threw it as far as I could, and waited to hear the plop as it hit the surface of the water.

I was walking briskly along an empty street; the houses on both sides seemed asleep. Suddenly three youngsters stepped out from the shadows and blocked my path. They were probably older than I and certainly stronger. I looked from one to the other. I had heard that in London the bodies of people who had been robbed and killed were thrown into the river.

"What do you want?" I asked, trying not to sound too frightened.

The three boys looked at me and then at each other. "He asks what we want," they said in unison as if it were a chant. Then the youngest of them said, "He is very kind." And the other two shook their heads and grinned.

"Let me pass!" I demanded and took a step forward.

"He wants to pass," one of them chided, as he pushed me back.

"I heard him," the youngest said, "but he has to pay duty. We collect ship money for the King."

"Let's take him to our captain," the biggest boy suggested, grabbing hold of my arms.

I tried to wrest myself free; but he laughed and tightened his grasp, and I realized that it was wiser not to resist. A handkerchief of some rough material was put around my head as a blind.

"Come," one of them said, as if I had a choice, as they pulled me forward.

Soon we entered a building and I was led up several flights of stairs. Finally, we stopped in front of a door, and one of the boys knocked on it.

Although I heard no answer, the door was flung open and I was pushed inside. I stumbled and fell. I heard many voices and the shuffling of feet; then the cloth that covered my eyes was untied and I stood up.

I was in a large room, in the middle of which was a table.

Around it were benches, except at the head, where there was a chair. The benches were so crowded that several boys had to stand.

In the single chair sat a youth with a curiously shriveled face. A candle cast its glare on his features. All fear left me. I recognized him. It was Ezra!

9
Ezra

————————

I had met Ezra a year ago at Worcester, where he had allowed me to join a group of about twenty boys whose captain he was. Not long after, that tiny army of children had been disbanded; but Ezra, his lieutenant William, Jack, and I had stayed together. At the Battle of Edgehill William had been killed. Finally, the three of us had come to London, but here Ezra had abandoned Jack and me, as soon as we entered the city.

The only light in that vast room was from the stub of a tallow candle; and since I was standing in the gloom, Ezra could not see me.

The expression on his face was not one of pleasure. "Who have you here? I told you I would have no one brought to this place!" His voice had become a shade deeper, but its pitch was still high.

"We found him almost on our doorstep. We thought his mother had deserted him and it was only Christian charity to shelter him. He has fine swaddling clothes ... Besides, he just begged to be brought along." It was the oldest of my captors who spoke. Neither his words nor his tone indicated any great respect for his captain.

"Poor Ezra," I thought, "forever wanting to rule and forever in danger of being deposed."

"If you wanted his clothes, why didn't you take them and let him run home to his mother in his skin?". Ezra's annoyance was great. While he spoke he glanced from one to the other of the boys near him to detect their reactions to this breach of his laws.

"His things are too small for me. He is hardly weaned yet," the youth replied; and though I could not see his face I knew it wore an arrogant expression. "But I thought you might like his clothes for yourself."

For a moment Ezra looked as if he might explode, like a pistol overloaded with powder. His face grew red and then pale, as though first the sun and then the moon had shone on it. But by an exercise of will, greater than I would have thought him capable, he kept his temper.

"I am captain here," he said loudly and very slowly, "and so long as I am, you shall obey me." He picked up a dagger that had been lying on the table and began to play with it. "I have my reasons for wishing no strangers brought here; and if you cannot guess them, you are even more of a fool than I thought you were."

While Ezra waited for the youngster to reply, he kept his gaze on him steadily. Finally, when several moments passed without anyone speaking, he shifted his glance to me.

I took a few steps forward. "Ezra!" I cried. "It's me, Oliver!"

"You!" Ezra looked as surprised as though I had risen from the grave. "I thought the rats had eaten you long ago." He did not seem pleased to see me; and only then did I recall that the last time I had seen him he was being beaten by his father. There had been a great crowd in the narrow London street watching the shoemaker hit his son with a leather strap; and poor Ezra had been weeping and cursing so piteously under the rain of blows that I had thought he could not have noticed me, but perhaps he had.

"The rats only nibbled at my toes. I am hale and hearty," I said warmly as I stepped up to the table. I held out my hand, but Ezra hesitated before he clasped it and told me to sit down.

"He was with me at Edgehill," he said. He looked at the other boys but not at me.

"That is where the dog is buried," I thought. "He has told a great many lies about that battle and he is afraid now of being found out."

"Is it true that of all the men in the army of Parliament Ezra was the swiftest runner, and that Prince Rupert did not even catch a glimpse of his arse?"

I did not need to turn around to know who had spoken. My captor's voice was familiar enough to me. "If you had been there," I said slowly, directing my gaze not at him but at the boys around the table, "I am sure you would have outrun us all. But until you have been in battle, it might be best for you not to boast of your abilities — no matter what they be — nor to belittle the courage of others."

At first I had thought of making a fool of the youth by making some coarse joke; but I quickly thought better of it, for in truth, I have never been fond of such nor good at telling them.

"What brings you to London?" Ezra's voice was deferential now. "And what good fortune has been yours?"

How tempted I was to say that I was a messenger for Colonel Cromwell and had brought important letters to London! But instead I muttered, "I am on the rolls of Major Whalley's regiment of horse."

The three boys who had captured me now came to the table. The others made room for them; they were obviously of some importance in Ezra's little army. I looked at them: Were they merely robbers and pickpockets who would leave their hands, if not their heads, on the executioner's block, or did they have ideals for which they wished to fight?

"Were you at Grantham?" one of them asked.

"No, but I was at Gainsborough," I replied; and I told them of the battle we had fought before we entered the town and of our retreat from it. I was careful not to brag because this was Ezra's weakness and I wanted them to know that I was not like their captain.

"Soon there will be no King," Ezra cried triumphantly. "Those who are now high will be brought low." He paused. "We have no more use for lords and kings than we do for bishops!"

Ezra's words I had heard before from others; and they sounded strange in his mouth, though he spoke most earnestly. I have met few who have had more of a liking for governing than he had; and he tried to rule as absolutely as King Charles himself, over anyone whom he could convince to follow him. I shrugged my shoulders; I would not argue politics with Ezra.

"It will come true." Ezra looked into the flame of the candle in front of him; and a dreamy expression changed his wrinkled, pock-marked face and made it almost handsome. "It will come true," he repeated.

"If many have his faith, it might," I thought, as I glanced at the faces of the youngsters seated at the table.

"I will become king!" a rosy-cheeked boy declared. He was one of the youngest among them and everyone laughed.

"Will you make me a duke?" one of the others asked.

"I will," said the younger boy. "I shall make you all dukes, and Ezra will be the General for all my armies."

"Thank you, Your Majesty," Ezra said. Although I do not think he liked the buffoonery, he did nothing to stop it.

I rose. I could see that the younger boys, at least, were in awe of me; and I no longer feared that they would try to rob me or hinder my departure.

"I will walk a bit of the way with you," Ezra announced to my surprise, after I said that I had to leave.

"They are fools, most of them," Ezra confided as soon as we were in the street. "I have not a lieutenant I can trust."

He sighed. "I miss William. He was worth the lot of them."

"Aye," I agreed. It was dark and I was glad that Ezra could not see my face. Poor William, I recalled how Ezra had snickered behind his back; even when he died after the battle of Edgehill, Ezra had not seemed to care. Yet it was true; William had been a most trusty lieutenant to him.

"Why don't you stay with me?"

Ezra's question seemed so absurd that I did not answer it.

"We have plenty of money," he said. "I can pay you better than any major."

"I am sure you could," I said and smiled, remembering how often I had not been paid. "But I am on the rolls of the regiment; that would be desertion."

"London is filled with deserters!" Ezra laughed. "For every man who joins the army, two run away."

I shook my head. It was not alone that what he said was madness; but I had no liking for these gangs which had sprung up since the war began and clothed themselves in some kind of legality by supporting either the King or Parliament.

"It is here in London, not in Cambridge, that all will be decided," Ezra argued heatedly. "Who rules London rules England!"

I thought of Colonel Cromwell and I decided that he would make short shrift of all the Ezras of this land; but somehow that was not a comforting thought either. Although the evening was warm, I shivered. Men were like the river rats, forever quarreling.

I held out my hand. We were nearing the house where I lodged. "We will meet again," I said as Ezra returned my grasp.

"I trust that you will tell no one where you found me," he said. "There are those who have no liking for me." He smiled proudly as if he had spoken of some honor that had been bestowed upon him.

I grinned. "Remember, I was blindfolded. Besides, I have nothing to tell."

"You shall hear of me!" Ezra boasted as he turned away.

"I shall," I thought. And somehow, it was this certainty which made me feel sorry for him.

10

Master John Selden

I found my two companions as cheerful as they had been when I left them that morning. The great city of London had proved less attractive to them than the humble house where they stayed. The shortest of walks was all they engaged in; and that had been only ventured upon in order to purchase ribbons for gifts to be given to the daughters of the house.

That evening was spent much as the former one had been. Some ale was drunk, some jokes were told, some songs were sung. Just as on the previous occasion, I did not partake in these simple pleasures, except for the ale which I sipped silently in a corner. I envied the two young troopers. Their fathers had owned land. In their childhood they had trod upon earth that was their own. They were contented. Let their world be confined within narrow borders; they had no wish to cross them. They had chosen to fight for Parliament; but having done that was enough philosophizing for their lifetime.

My mind wandered to Ezra and Master Waldon. I had not told my comrades or my hosts of my adventures that day. Suddenly there was a particularly loud burst of laughter and I thought, "If these two young men had been in London during the rioting, could they have been part of the mob who invaded Master Waldon's house and killed his daughter?" I wanted to answer yes; but then I felt ashamed for having phrased the question at all. You cannot judge anyone for what you think he might have done, not even yourself.

The next morning I was up early. There were clouds in the sky but it was not raining. I told my escort that I hoped we should be able to leave shortly after noon. They were much disappointed; they had hoped to stay a few days more. At no point had they shown any interest in what my letters might contain or whom they were for. Or perhaps — though I did not think of it then — they found me too taciturn to approach with such queries.

I went first to Lincoln's Inn to wait upon Oliver St. John. He had already written a letter for Colonel Cromwell and I was called at once into his study to receive it.

Oliver St. John was a man of importance, a Member of Parliament who was much respected. But he was dour. "If his outside is any reflection of what is within him, then he is a Puritan," I thought.

He asked me several questions about the army, most of which had to do with pay. I was able to answer readily enough and one of my replies was greeted with a thin smile. "If a trooper's stomach rumbles too loud, he cannot hear the commands of his officers," I explained.

I was eager to be off, as I had been told to wait upon Master John Selden at White Friars by ten. Yet I could not take my leave from Oliver St. John until I was dismissed. Finally, when my impatience was making it almost impossible for me to stand still, some other visitor was announced, and having handed me his letter, Oliver St. John briskly ordered me to depart.

This time when I arrived at White Friars, I was taken to a small room, the walls of which were lined with books. Master Selden was seated at a table. Before him were several volumes, some open and some closed, besides a great confusion of papers. When he saw me, he took a cloth and covered all this disarray; then he asked me to sit down across from him. Obediently, I sat on the edge of the chair and waited for him to speak.

"I have a letter here for Major Whalley; whether he will be satisfied with it is another matter. He asks a good many questions." Master Selden smiled. "Are all the soldiers of the army of Parliament as philosophical as your master?"

"I don't know," I answered. "But there are many who like to talk about more than the weather."

"And I warrant you are one of them." Pursing his lips, Master Selden looked at me quizzically. "What is your name?"

"Oliver . . . Oliver Cutter," I added quickly.

"You are very young to be a messenger. What is your age?"

"Sixteen," I said, and blushed because it was a lie.

Master Selden mistook the flush; he thought that it was caused by my shame at my youth. "Of all the transient gifts we shall ever possess, youth is the most precious and the one which causes us the most embarrassment. We never appreciate it until it is lost; and then we discover that however much we search for it, we shall never find it again."

"Most older people find it a great fault in one, that one is young," I said and looked away.

"Aye, Oliver, you have hit the mark there, for the crime of youth is youth itself. But if you use it well you might — when your own locks are gray — tolerate this crime in your children."

"I shall remember that, sir," I said, although at the same time, I wondered whether youth, in truth, was something that could be spent either ill or well. It seemed to me that I had not had much choice over mine.

"You must know the army well . . . being a courier." Master Selden looked at me thoughtfully. "I have been told that some of the troops of Colonel Cromwell call themselves 'Saints.' That is a strange title for a soldier. Is it true?"

"Aye, there are some who do, but it is not common." I recalled the trooper I had met at the battle of Gainsborough. "I think they belong to a particular sect. I don't know which one, but they are much against swearing."

"There are more ways than a curse of taking the Lord's

name in vain." Master Selden sighed. "We may be depos-
ing one despot just to set up another, who will care as much
for power and as little for law."

"That is true, sir." I was thinking of Ezra. Certainly he
would be a despot, if he had power. "But the cause of
Parliament . . ."

"Words, young man!" Master Selden interrupted me;
then, glancing at my sword, he said, "What is your cause?
Surely you must have one, if you wear a weapon. For if
you do not then you are merely a ruffian, who likes the
sight of blood."

I blushed, half with shame and half out of annoyance.
"I have no liking for fighting, sir," I muttered.

"All will say that, but what they mean is that they have
no liking for getting killed." Master Selden smiled. "The
Scots Presbyterians have their 'cause,' but it is no more mine
than is the King's."

"Nor is it mine," I agreed fervently.

"To me the cause of Parliament is liberty . . . Liberty
above all," he said dreamily, looking down at his table, as
if liberty itself lay there underneath the cloth.

"Liberty," I whispered. I knew the word. But what in
truth was it? Could it be the same for Ezra as for me?

"Liberty to speak and think and write, to live a free man
under the law. To govern ourselves through Parliament."
Master Selden let his gaze rest upon me. "Though you may
not be able to write or read, young man, you can speak.
We want no honestly spoken word deemed treason to suit

a tyrant. We want Parliament to make the laws which must govern the nation. We want taxes determined by Parliament's will, not by Royal whims or needs."

I nodded. I thought I understood. It sounded good and had been finely said. Had I dared I would have told Master Selden about my friend Jack. Jack, too, had read many books and could speak well; he had even known Latin.

"Free men governing themselves by reason and justice." Master Selden almost whispered the words, as if he, himself, felt embarrassed by having to say them aloud.

"But what if that is not what *they* want?" I asked in almost as low a tone; whom I meant by *they* I was not quite sure of myself; but Master Selden seemed to understand.

"Then we shall have tyranny," he replied and smiled sourly. "Saints with swords, and church elders who are worse than bishops." He knotted one of his hands into a fist and drove it into the palm of the other. "We may jump from the frying pan into the fire. But no despot lasts forever. No matter how saintly he is, age will crack his bones." He shook his head. "Presbyters and saints." Then suddenly he smiled almost gaily. "You can tell Major Whalley that as for the Solemn League and Covenant, it best be taken like a doctor's pill: swallowed whole rather than chewed."

"Yes, sir," I said, although I thought that the Major would be disappointed.

"And what sect do you belong to, Oliver Cutter? What

grand truth have you spelled out of the Bible?" Master Selden looked at me expectantly.

"None, sir," I answered truthfully.

"Well, that is just as well, for sects are like cages. Once inside you will never be free to fly again." Master Selden rose and handed me his letter to Major Whalley. "Yet they have their attraction . . . these cages. They must have, since so many people desire to spend their lives inside them. Their faith is safe when iron bars keep out doubt . . . But not admirable!" Master Selden had walked with me as far as the door. "Faith must not fear doubt, but rejoice in it and grow strong from battling with it."

I knew these final words were spoken not for me but for himself. Yet I took them to heart. My trouble was that my faith was so small and my doubts so many. Yet never in my life have I felt so proud, as I did that day, when I stood in the street in front of White Friars. The wisest man in England had spoken to me almost as if I were his equal.

11
Scholar Oliver

A messenger is much concerned about the contents of the letters he carries. If they be pleasing to him who receives them, the messenger is often rewarded; but if he carries bad news, then he might as well prepare himself for a wintry reception. The letter which I brought to Colonel Cromwell from Oliver St. John was so much to his liking that he gave me two shillings; and from Major Whalley I received three.

"And you saw him, Oliver?" he asked eagerly.

When I told Major Whalley of my conversation with Master John Selden, he declared that he envied me and wished he had gone to London himself. Then I recited Master Selden's advice about the Solemn League and Covenant.

"Like the doctor's pill," the Major repeated and laughed. It was at this point that he gave me the three shillings.

The money I could not keep because I owed more than five shillings to the widow with whom I lodged. I think she was pleased, for she was a poor woman, but she made a show of not caring whether she was paid or not. I wondered whether this were because of her pride or her love of Parliament. The thought that she might have some affection for me did not occur to me then.

A few days after my return from London, I was sent by Major Whalley to Cambridge with a letter to a lieutenant. It was a message of no importance, but it was to cause me great embarrassment.

When I was shown into the officer's room, he was dressing and read the letter hastily; then he asked me whether I could write. An honest reply would have been, no. Although I could write my name, I had difficulty linking the letters together, and I had hardly ever written anything else. But pride made me say yes; and while the lieutenant shaved, he dictated a letter for Major Whalley.

If the young officer had seen the strange markings I made upon that piece of paper, he would have laughed or been angry; in either case, he would have written the letter himself. But since it was of no importance, containing only some information about supplies, and someone came just as he was finishing, he ordered me to return to Major Whalley without so much as glancing at the paper.

The ride from Cambridge to our headquarters in Huntingdon was long enough for me to have ample time to ponder what to do: but I arrived without having reached any conclusion. Short messages were often given verbally, especially in the field; but if I pretended that the lieutenant had told me what to say, Major Whalley might be offended. He had himself written to the younger officer, and when next they met, he might tax the lieutenant for lack of courtesy. Yet I could not give the note to the Major without explaining the unusual script.

With much misgiving, I told the Major's servant that I wished to speak with his master; but when I stood before him, I handed him the letter without saying a word.

The Major looked at it long and then shook his head. "My Greek is so poor, I cannot read it," he said laughingly.

"I . . . I wrote it, sir . . . and I cannot write!" I finally stammered.

"Then you must translate, Oliver," he said and gave me back the letter.

I took the miserable document in my hands. With all the blots of ink I had made each time I had dipped the wretched quill, it looked even worse than I remembered it. I started to read, but soon tears of humiliation started to run from my eyes and I stopped.

Major Whalley ceased laughing and gave me a handkerchief.

I dried my eyes and read the note to the end. When I had finished, the Major held out his hand for the letter. As he glanced at it once more, I saw him grin, though he tried to hide it.

I had acted like a fool. If I had told the lieutenant that I could not write, he would not have given it a second thought, for few of the troopers could write more than their own names. To boast of an accomplishment I did not possess reminded me of my father; he was just such a donkey as to do this all the time. "But he, at least, can write," I thought.

That night I lay awake thinking about my father; and although I swore to myself many times that I would not be like him, I could not help feeling sorry for him as well as for myself.

My humiliation had a result which I had not expected. The very next day, Major Whalley told me that he had made arrangements for me to be taught how to read and write by a curate who was attached to our regiment and preached in the Church of St. John.

It was with much fear that I attended my first lesson. Most of all, I was afraid that the Reverend Sparrow would laugh because he found me such a dunce that I was not worthy of his teaching. But the Reverend Sparrow, true to his name, was no hawk ready to pounce on poor Oliver Cutter. He treated me kindly, though he was a strict master and expected his pupils to work; and this I did.

During the day I was a messenger for Major Whalley, but I was never sent far afield. The evenings were my own, and these I spent in study. Often I sat before my table in the attic until late into the night, filling sheets of paper with rudely written lines. Slowly the mysterious signs became recognizable letters. I also learned how to cut a goose feather into a pen with which I could make a line as fine as a hair.

As to reading, I needed only practice and the Reverend Sparrow lent me his Bible. Soon I realized that this great book contained more than the admonitions and threats of hell's fires which my father's misuse of it had led me to believe. It is also the history of a people. Being wise, my teacher chose those passages which he knew would interest a youngster to examine me in. The story which I liked best was that of Saul and David. When he questioned me about it, I confessed that I had felt sorry for Saul, although I knew that he was wrong.

"If you could not grieve for King Saul, there would be no tragedy in his history," he explained.

The Reverend Sparrow was a Puritan and had little use for those activities which he deemed worldly. He saw our life as a trial with God in the judgment seat. Amusements such as dancing or games of any kind, he found not only a frivolous waste of time, but also a danger to your soul. They were stepping stones on the road to Perdition. But like many another Puritan, he had his weakness. Colonel Cromwell was fond of music; the Reverend Sparrow's failing was a love of poetry. It is the mark of a good man that what he loves he needs to share, and in this my teacher was no different.

Shyly, after one of my lessons had gone well, he read a poem to me by Master John Milton called "Lycidas." When he finished he asked me whether I liked it. I do not recall what I replied, only that it was not the truth, for I had understood very little of it. How could a boy as ignorant

71

as I was make any meaning out of such ravings? It was packed with more words that I did not understand than a pudding with plums. Yet there were phrases which moved me. "Fame is the spur" ... "Look homeward Angel" ... They have stayed in my mind, though I cannot explain why.

Whatever I said, it did not dampen the Reverend Sparrow's enthusiasm. When the next lesson was finished, he read several poems to me by John Donne, who had been a clergyman. I did not understand these any better than I had Master Milton's poem, but they were like music, like a song I enjoyed listening to.

It became my teacher's habit to read poetry aloud after every lesson; and he served it with the same pride that a man uncorks a bottle of rare wine.

Almost all the poems were concerned with God and our need for salvation from this sinful world. The Reverend Sparrow worried much about the souls left in his charge and felt most deeply his responsibility. Yet one evening he read to me some sonnets by Master Shakespeare; and as he did so, two tears ran down his cheek. When he finished, he wiped them away and blushed. These were the first poems which he had read to me that I understood, and I asked him if I might make a copy of them. He gave his permission reluctantly, and yet I could see that he was pleased.

When next I came to him, I showed him what I had done. It was the prettiest writing of which I was capable: each line was straight and the letters were almost all the same size. The Reverend Sparrow complimented my work, but it seemed to make him ill at ease.

"Unhappily, Master Shakespeare was a worldling," he said sadly. "He used the great gift which the Lord had given him to purposes not worthy of it. He wrote for the theater! And as you know, Oliver, the theater is Satan's temple!"

I had seen only one play; but I had met an actor twice, and liked him even more on the second occasion than on the first, so I did not share the Reverend Sparrow's hatred of the theater. His opinion, though, was common among those who supported the cause of Parliament, and the theaters of London had been ordered closed for more than a year.

"Oh, Oliver, what could Master Shakespeare not have done for the work of the Lord, if he had turned his talent to His cause and preached us sermons that would have been like the words of angels!"

To this I agreed, though silently I thought that I would like to read these plays that Master Shakespeare had written.

As I progressed in my skills, my ambitions grew and I was contemplating asking the Reverend Sparrow to teach me Latin, for it seems you cannot call yourself educated unless you know that language. But my life as a scholar had hardly begun when it abruptly stopped. Had it continued there would have been less of a tale to tell; I might now be living in Cambridge instead of this rude town in the wilderness. But a twig in the river is driven by the currents; the water is its master.

12
The Spy

———————

December 1643 was a cold month. Winter had come early, blowing its icy breath all over England. At Vinceby, in October, Parliament had won a great victory. The Scots had taken part in the battle; but if a single unit and a single man should be called victor, it was our cavalry regiment and its captain, Colonel Cromwell. I had not been at Vinceby, but I had heard veterans describe what happened there often enough. In truth, all battles are alike: one side slaughters the other; but the same rage, fear, and horror are experienced by all, victor as well as vanquished. It is only afterwards, in the chimney corner, that the glory is felt.

It had snowed during the night; and I was up so early that the world was yet unused. The streets of Huntingdon were covered by a white blanket which only birds had trod upon. The sky was clear and the sun just rising. I went first to see to my horse, which was stabled not far from my own quarters. She stuck her face into mine and her muzzle touched my nose. Her skin was as soft as velvet; her breath was warm and had a pleasant smell. I fondled her and then

I went to fetch a bucket of water to give her a drink. Of all the animals that we master, there is none we take a greater pleasure in serving than the horse. I have seen men whom I thought had no tender feelings at all stand watching their horses eat with a smile on their faces, not unlike the one a mother has when she feeds her babe.

By the time this duty was finished, the town was awake. As I returned to my lodgings for my breakfast, I met many a passer-by, his steps muted by the snow. I hoped that I would be sent on a journey that day, for it was such fine weather for a ride. The Colonel, who had been in London attending to the business of Parliament, had returned a few days ago and was now in Ely. As I ate my porridge, I imagined the beautiful cathedral all covered with snow, and I was eager to see it.

At headquarters, I was told that Major Whalley wanted to see me. Cornet Wilkins was with him when I arrived, and I posted myself near the door. I was used to standing quietly unnoticed, and more often than not I did not pay any attention to what the officers said or did, but that morning, I could not help listening. The fine weather and the approaching holiday season had made the two young men lighthearted and they laughed a great deal.

"Abolish Christmas!" Cornet Wilkins exclaimed, astounded.

"The Scottish Presbyterians have proposed in Parliament that Christmas should be an ordinary working day," Major Whalley explained. "Have no fear, it will never be passed.

But think how unpopular the Scots will become because they suggested it."

This prospect seemed to delight both the officers. I could not have agreed more with them, for, to an Englishman, Christmas is the merriest holiday in the year, celebrated not only by attendance at church and prayers, but also by the grandest of meals, when even the poor eat like lords.

After Cornet Wilkins had left, Major Whalley looked at me with a puzzled air, as if he did not know why I was there.

"You must be in Ely by the afternoon. Colonel Cromwell wishes to see you," he finally said.

For a moment he seemed about to say something more, and I waited expectantly. But he only shook his head and smiled; then, just as I was leaving, he asked me how my studies were progressing.

With a burst of pride, I said that they were going well; and I hoped to ask the Reverend Sparrow to teach me Latin.

I had feared that Major Whalley might laugh, but he didn't; he spoke to me very seriously. "There's many a fool who knows Latin and many a wise man only English. Who knows which lessons are the most important, those learned from books or those the world teaches us?"

I was very disappointed that he did not approve of my plan, and I think my face showed it.

"We must all make sacrifices for Parliament, Oliver . . ." Suddenly he smiled. "Latin would not be the hardest one for me to make. It is but ballast and not necessary to a man loaded with experience."

I did not reply but only nodded, for a strange uneasiness had crept over me. Major Whalley knew something concerning me which I didn't, and I suspected that it was not pleasant.

During my ride to Ely, I turned his words over and over in my mind. First I pondered the possibility that the Reverend Sparrow might be at the root of it — perhaps he did not want to teach me any longer. But he had been so friendly the last time he gave me a lesson. It was his very praise that had made me want to ask him to teach me Latin. No, that idea had to be dismissed.

Soon, in spite of my preoccupations, I was enjoying the ride. Seldom have I seen the fenland look lovelier. By noon, the sun had enough strength to make some of the snow melt; and all the little streams I passed gurgled as if they were laughing. Everyone greeted me cheerfully; on such a merry morning only the most miserable of men could keep from smiling. My mare showed her spirits by continually breaking into a canter, and I swear, had she had her way, we would have galloped from Huntingdon to Ely.

When we arrived, I rode around the cathedral before taking my horse to the Colonel's stables. There are grander cathedrals in England but they are too often cramped by other buildings. The town of Ely is hardly more than a village; and the cathedral, like a beautiful young maiden from whom the plain homespun girls keep their distance, stands alone. While I marveled at its beauty, I thought that when man constructed a house of God, it was the godly part of him that did design and build it.

As soon as I presented myself at the Colonel's house, I was led into his presence. It was the same room where I had first set eyes upon Oliver Cromwell, and the setting was very like that of our first meeting. On that day, too, a roaring fire had burned on the hearth, and the Colonel had not been alone. But whereas then his guest had been Major Whalley, another man now stood beside him and warmed his hands by the fire. I recognized him. It was Major Ireton, who had fought at Gainsborough. Then he had only been a captain. As a man he was brave and as an officer much respected; but unlike Major Whalley, he was not loved by the troopers. Nature had stamped his features in a stern mold; there were no wrinkles around his deep-set eyes or straight mouth to tattle tales of hidden laughter.

Both men had turned to look at me when I entered the room. The Colonel smiled, but Major Ireton studied me as I have seen men do when they were judging whether a horse were worthy of the price being asked for it.

"Come closer, Oliver," the Colonel said. He indicated a low stool near him.

I had never before sat down in the Colonel's presence, and I would have preferred to stand. As I sat at the very edge of the stool, my eyes darted from the Colonel to Major Ireton, who had remained by the fire.

"Cousin Whalley tells me that your writing has so improved that he can now read it at first glance." The Colonel's grin made me suspect that he knew all about my first unfortunate effort. "This skill of yours will be of use to us." The Colonel seemed to be trying to meet Major Ireton's glance, but the latter still kept his gaze on me.

"Colonel Cromwell has informed me that you know Oxford," he said.

"Yes, sir," I answered.

"That you have been there before and that not long ago." Major Ireton's voice was always intense, as if the words within him were waiting to leap from his mouth. "Good. As you know, it is the King's headquarters," he continued without even waiting for me to nod. "Now King Charles is going to call a parliament there, as if the one in Westminster were not the lawful body to govern this land."

"The war is like a game of chess, Oliver," Colonel Cromwell interrupted. "The King makes his move and we, ours; though the chessmen are not wooden figures but flesh and blood, and therefore we cannot rely upon them always to stay in their squares."

"But we, unlike the King, play the game without bishops." Major Ireton almost laughed.

"So we do," the Colonel agreed, "and that is why we make better use of our pawns. Knights jump about too much for our taste ... No pawns will win this game, for they cannot move backwards."

I tried to make sense out of the words bandied about by

the two officers. I had heard of the game of chess; it was the only one of which the Reverend Sparrow approved, and he had shown me the curious ways the figures moved across the board. "In chess, the men cannot change sides; white cannot become black," I said.

"I told you, Henry," the Colonel smiled towards the Major, "that Oliver is not a fool. His head is stuck on his neck for more than consuming porridge."

"Yes, I think he will do." Major Ireton looked at me so grimly that I thought he was reluctant to agree with the Colonel. "Anyone who has eyes in his head can see, but to observe demands something more. We are going to send you to Oxford."

"You will be carrying letters to friends there," Colonel Cromwell said very seriously. "We do have those we can trust within those gates."

When Colonel Cromwell paused, Major Ireton spoke, "But how many and who our friends are, we are not sure."

"Yes, Oliver, you will be delivering letters; but we want you to stay in Oxford and study all who attend the King's parliament. It is a dangerous mission and one which I am not sure will succeed. We will give you the name of one we trust, who will smuggle out any messages you may write."

Now I recalled the expression on Major Whalley's face that morning. "He knew," I thought, "and he did not like it." My voice trembled when I spoke aloud, "Am I to be a spy, sir?"

The Colonel looked away; he knew well what happened

to spies when they were caught. It was Major Ireton who replied, "Some deem that profession shameful, but it is vanity to set even one's honor above the cause of God."

"I would rather send someone else," Colonel Cromwell finally turned to me again, "but you carry your own disguise."

"Who notices a boy?" Major Ireton added energetically. "You can flit in and out of every kitchen without being more conspicuous than a sparrow in a stable."

"My daughter told me that you have been in the Royal kitchen at Oxford," Colonel Cromwell remarked.

"Most servants know their masters' secrets," Major Ireton continued. "There are few among them who are not gossips, so listen well to everything you hear."

"When am I to go, sir?" I asked, knowing I had no choice.

"In a few weeks; there is much to arrange," the Major said curtly.

"But are you not hungry, Oliver?" the Colonel's tone was almost apologetic. "Come," he said as he rose. "Let us go and find Bettie. She is sure to have saved something good for you, for you are her favorite."

Never before had Colonel Cromwell called his daughter Bettie when speaking to me of her. I had been hungry when I arrived in Ely, but now I was no longer.

13

The Scottish Laird

A thaw had set in. The fields were still covered by snow, but the road that stretched in front of me was a thin path of yellow mud. My horse was breathing deeply, and its flanks were wet with sweat. I was not riding my own horse but a broken-winded gelding, whose mane was flecked with gray. The poor animal had once been a fine horse and when I had saddled it in the morning, it had shown some spirit, but soon age tamed it. I was on my way to Aylesbury, the outpost of the Parliamentary army in the west; and since whatever horse transported me there would never see Huntingdon again, I had been given this poor nag.

It was four weeks after my conversation with Colonel Cromwell and Major Ireton. Since then I had met the Major many times, and now as my horse plodded its way wearily through the mud, I had more than enough time to ponder over those strange conclaves.

I both liked and disliked Major Ireton. One moment his fervent faith in Parliament convinced me that its cause was the most righteous in the world; but in the next, some hidden cunning in the man was exposed which made me doubt his sincerity. Yet the Oliver who rode that morning towards Aylesbury was not only Cromwell's boy, he had another title as well: Major Ireton's spy.

My mission to Oxford was more than to deliver letters. I was to spy on certain members of the parliament which the King had called. This parliament was a ruse to fool the people, for Charles never meant it to have any power. Yet among those who had accepted his invitations to Oxford were some worthy men.

"What we want to know" — Major Ireton never said "I" — "is whether they are acting alone, on their own initiatives, or for someone else."

"And who would that be, sir?" I had asked.

The Major had smiled his usual smile which had no merriment in it; then he had lowered his voice almost to a whisper, although we were alone and none could have heard him had he shouted. "We want especially to know if they have any connection with the Earl of Essex."

I must have hidden my amazement better than I dared hope I could. "The hero of Edgehill," I had thought. "The nobleman whom poor William, Ezra's lieutenant, had dreamed was his unknown father. Then, no man had been more loved and respected by our army than the Earl of Essex."

Now, riding all alone in the gray winter landscape, it

struck me how divided the supporters of the cause of Parliament must be when a Colonel and a Major would spy on and plot against their own general.

A rider feels the wishes of his steed, as if the animal's body were an extension of his own. My horse was tired, and I should have stopped for the night at Shefford, but I wanted to push on to the village of Ampthill. I had been there before, and I knew that there was an inn used by cattle drovers, where not too many questions were asked.

Suddenly the horse stood still. I kicked its flanks and it took a few steps and then stopped once more. I jumped to the ground to see what was the matter. The gelding turned its head and looked at me with its big dark brown eyes that seemed to say, "I am sorry — I am too old for this."

I took the bridle in my hand and trudged on, leading the horse as if it were a dog being taken for a walk. It was getting dark, and now it was cold enough for the melted snow to freeze and make the road icy. In the west were clouds that told that we might have snow before the night was over. I walked briskly; my poor horse stumbling behind me.

The first flakes of snow were falling when I entered Ampthill, and I longed for the warm tavern of the inn as much as my poor nag longed for the stable. The weather being bad and the holiday season over, there were few travelers, and I was given a room to myself; had the inn been crowded I should have had to bargain in order to share a bed.

I paid the stable boy a shilling to wipe down my old

gelding and feed it properly with both oats and hay, though I warned the boy not to give the horse too many oats as they can give colic after a long ride. I, having a young stomach which was as empty as a beggar's bag on a rainy day, did not fear filling it. I ordered chops and warm ale; and when the girl who served me said that there was fowl to be had, I told her to bring me that as well.

In the center of the room was the usual long table with benches around it, but the young maid showed me to a smaller one where I might dine alone. This had both advantages and disadvantages. At the larger table I would be noticed only for as long as it would take me to tell the farmers who were sitting there where I came from and where I was going. But seated in state, alone, I would be the object of interest.

I was already eating my meal when one of the men from the other table finally could no longer keep his curiosity in check. I put down the leg of the chicken on which I had been gnawing and looked at the farmer carefully. His face was flushed and his small narrow eyes measured me without much sympathy, as he mumbled his question.

"I have come from Huntingdon," I replied and picked up my drumstick. I thought he was going to return to his companions with this information, for he turned away from me; but then he thought better of it and asked me where I was going.

"If the snow be not too heavy, I aim to be in Aylesbury by tomorrow," I said, keeping the tone of voice polite yet not overly friendly. For one wild moment I had thought of saying Oxford just to see the expression on his face. It frightened me that such foolishness could even cross my mind.

"There'll be a pile of snow falling before the night is over." The farmer sniffed. "It's not much of a nag you be riding."

I agreed with him and grinned, for I realized that he and his companions had all been at the window when I entered the courtyard of the inn, and I could readily imagine the comments my poor mount had caused. The farmer wrinkled his brow; he was trying very hard to find something more to say, but he couldn't. With a nod, he returned to the other table.

When I had finished my meal, I took my tankard of ale to the fireplace and toasted my feet. I was now so close to their table that the farmers could include me in their conversation by raising their voices only a little.

"You would not be from Cromwell's regiment?" a younger man asked in such a friendly tone that I judged it wise to say yes.

"I have no use for either side," the farmer who had approached me first now declared. "They both steal your horses."

"I think that the Colonel has paid for every bit of horse-flesh his men ride," I said, while, with my knife, I scraped some of the mud off my boots and threw it into the fire.

"He did not pay many shillings for yours," a fat, jolly man, who had not spoken before, remarked.

"He was cheated," I rejoined, draining the last of my ale.

I was just about to go to my room, when a tall man with a soldierly bearing entered. His clothes were almost threadbare but they were well cut. "God's peace," he said and walked straight up to the fire. No one answered his greeting. Glancing at the faces of the farmers, I realized that the newcomer was as much a stranger to them as I was.

"This is weather that would suit a Russian, but it is not fit for a Christian." The tall man held out his hands and the heavy veins on the backs of them told more of a tale than his face, which was almost lost in shadow; it was many winters since he had been young.

"Is it true, sir, that the Russians have hair all over their bodies like bears and that they never cook their meat?" This was asked by the fat man, whose pale face made me think that he might be a miller.

"Aye," agreed the stranger, although he winked at me before he turned to face the men at the table. "The Russians in the north do, but those from the south have fur like cats. I like the northerners best because though they eat their meat raw I have never seen them eat children."

I could hear the others gasp. Now *there* was news worth telling when they went home. "You have been there, sir?"

"Aye, as far as Novgorod with the King." The soldier grunted as if he had thought of something unpleasant.

"And what would the King be doing in such heathen places?" the youngest of the men asked.

The tall man laughed. "I talk not of that dwarf in Oxford but of the great King Gustav Adolphus of Sweden. I fought with him in Russia and I was at his side at the Battle of Lutzen, when he was killed. No greater king has ever lived, and many a Scots laird like myself has served him."

The young maid, who was taking away my empty plates, turned for a moment to look at the Scot and her glance asked him if he wanted meat and drink. The Laird seemed to avoid her gaze and I thought, "He has not two pennies in his purse to rub together."

"Would you join me in a pot of ale?" I offered, while I cautioned myself to watch my tongue. There was something about the man that I did not trust. Although I had heard the King of Sweden had had many Scots in his army, I doubted that there were more than a few lairds; and as for his bragging about his services in foreign wars, such stories were familiar to me from others.

"It is always pleasing to drink with one's peers." The Scottish nobleman smiled and made a little bow.

I returned his courtesy, thinking that he was probably right — we were equals. He had screamed his first cry in some shepherd's hut in the highlands which had not been much better than the hovel that had been my ancestral home.

The thirst of my Scottish friend was of proportions that suited his height. I drank little but listened much. I believe that every story he told was a lie; and yet I am sure that he had experienced enough of life to hold forth a whole winter in the chimney corner without needing to bend the truth. I think he preferred lying. It was an old habit and those are the hardest to be rid of.

What amused me more were the farmers and the way they doted on his every word. These men, who in their daily lives were so mistrustful that they would not buy a sheep from each other without fear of being cheated, sat with their mouths open, like a bunch of simpletons, believing every outrageous story the soldier told them, as if it were the gospel truth.

It was almost midnight when I ordered the last pot of ale for the old soldier and then begged to be excused. The farmers were still listening to him.

I went to the stable to see how my horse was faring. It was lying down and I wished it a good night's rest, while I hoped that it would be able to stand in the morning. It was snowing heavily; but there was no wind, so it wouldn't form drifts.

14

Thievery

I woke in the morning just as the window of my room was turning pale gray. I jumped out of bed in my shirt and ran to see what the world looked like. It was still snowing, and my bare feet on the floor told me it was cold. Quickly I slipped back into bed and buried myself in its warmth.

It would be hopeless to attempt to travel farther with my old nag before it stopped snowing. I wondered where the Scottish Laird had slept. Had he been able to convince the inn-keeper to give him a place to rest? It had been cunning of me to buy him a pot of ale and then retire myself before he had had time to drink it, for I had been afraid that he might ask to share my bed.

There was a knock on the door. It had no lock on it, and I had put a chair against it, so that anyone who tried to get into my room during the night would awaken me. I had more money with me than I had ever owned before in my life. I felt under my pillow; the purse was still there and as heavy as ever. I had also sewn two golden sovereigns into the seams of my shirt. I called out and asked who was there before I drew the chair away.

Just as I dived back into bed, the young girl who had served me the night before opened the door. She had been sent to ask me what I wanted for breakfast and whether I should like a bowl of warm milk before I rose.

"Aye," I said and blushed, for I feared that she might have seen me in only my shirt.

She grinned back. We were about the same age. While she was gone, I combed my hair with my fingers.

"That old soldier you drank with left in the middle of the night," she said as she gave me the warm milk. Her cheeks were dimpled from suppressed laughter.

"It was a cold night to go a-wandering." I was a little disappointed. I knew that I would be spending the day at the inn, and I should have been glad for the company of the Scot.

"He took two pewter tankards and some plates as well. He tried to steal your horse, but the boy who sleeps in the stable heard him." The girl started to laugh. "I think he was so hungry that he could have eaten me uncooked just as the Russians eat children."

The thought of the Scottish Laird alone in the snowstorm carrying pewter tableware was both amusing and a little sad. Although he might have been humbly born, I believed that he had been used to command in that Swedish king's army, and it must have held hard with his pride, for him to act the common thief.

"My master is as mad as a bull this morning," the maid

said merrily. She found the inn-keeper's rage a matter for mirth.

A day at an inn is very long when the weather is such that you cannot even stick your nose outside. Minutes stretch like hours, and you have time for thought. But my poor horse was grateful for the day of rest, and I made certain that it was decently fed.

For a short while I talked with the inn-keeper. He told me that he was for Parliament; but most inn-keepers are weathervanes who like to please their customers. It was a wonder to me how a war could sweep across England like a storm, and affect so little the thoughts of most men. They treated the war like the weather — it was something over which they had no control. You saved what you could and if there was a profit to be made, you took it. This you thanked God for and the rest you blamed on the devil.

Seated in front of the fire in the tavern, I daydreamed of the reception I would receive in Oxford. So much had happened to me in the year that had passed since Jack and I had left that town to carry a message to Colonel Cromwell. I was not the same boy. I smiled to myself, remembering what a foolish child I had been. I had been frightened of the inn-keeper we had stayed with, because he was a hunchback; and although Jack had been my only friend, I had been in awe of him. Now I would be his equal. It never occurred to me that the year which had so changed my life could have changed theirs as well.

I saw myself opening the door of the Unicorn, Master Powers's inn, and finding everything exactly as it had been. Faith, his daughter, would run to meet me. Jack, who had been wounded by the highwaymen almost at the beginning of our journey to Cambridge, would be well; and in my daydream, he, too, would be at the inn when I returned. Such thoughts are sweet, and during that day I was snowbound in Ampthill, I imagined the same scene over and over again.

The next morning, the sky was blue. There was not even a breath of wind to disturb the snow lying on the branches of the trees. When I paid my reckoning, the inn-keeper, still mourning the loss of his pewter, asked me whether I thought the Scot was a King's man.

Although I suspected that if the Laird was on anyone's side but his own, it was probably Parliament's, there is no point in soiling your own nest, so I replied, yes. This was not a lie, for I had not mentioned which "king" I believed the Scot served, and he had been long in King Gustav Adolphus's army.

"May the plague strike any man who enters an inn without silver in his purse to pay!" The inn-keeper grumbled; and I laughed to myself, thinking that his words might well do as a motto for all the inn-keepers in the whole world.

As I rode away, I saw the young serving girl waving from a window. She had opened it and was leaning out. I doffed my hat and made a flourish with it. On such a fine morning, it would be shameful not to be happy.

The sun was setting as I came within sight of Aylesbury. Had I been on my own mare I would have been there hours earlier. I was stopped by the forepost of the garrison, about a mile before the town; but when I told the officer that I carried a message from Colonel Cromwell to Colonel Mosley, I was given an escort to accompany me to headquarters.

Aylesbury was poorly fortified, although guns had been placed so that they commanded the road and some barricades had been constructed. The garrison was large, but it consisted mainly of foot soldiers. The troops were much more disorderly than those of Colonel Cromwell, and I saw several men who were the worse for drink.

The house where Colonel Mosley was quartered was a fine one. I gave the letter which I carried for him to a young officer, who came back within a few minutes to tell me that I should wait upon his Colonel the following morning. Politely, I asked the lieutenant if he knew where I might find lodging for the night; he hardly bothered to listen to me and did not trouble himself to answer.

There were soldiers everywhere. Only at an inn called "The Bell" was I offered anything at all: a bed that I would have to share with two strangers. Finally I found a barn which would house both my poor nag and me. I preferred a bed of straw in the corner of a stable: I might be bitten by fleas in both places, but I stood less of a chance of being robbed so long as I stuck to the company of horses.

15
Colonel Mosley

"You will find Oxford changed." Colonel Mosley smiled. "The King has more fear of us and keeps the town like a fortress. If you should be caught, I cannot recommend Oxford Castle; it is a poor place to lodge. As for the inn-keeper, his name is Provost Marshal Smith and it is said that the devil's grandmother gave birth to him after having lain with her own grandson."

I grinned to show that I appreciated the Colonel's wit. Oxford Castle was an ancient building now only used as a prison, and I declared that I would keep well away from it.

"You will be wise to do that. For, jesting aside, that man has no heart. Methinks he was born with a lump of lead in his chest. It is but a month ago that I lost to him my best ears in that city. Like a little mouse he listened to all. He even had a mouse hole in the King's bedchamber. When we lost him, we lost not only the best spy we ever had, but the only honest inn-keeper in Oxford."

"Master Powers!" I gasped. I saw his face in front of me: his lively eyes and fine head that sat on his hunched shoulders as if he had no neck at all.

"You knew him?" Colonel Mosley sounded surprised.

"He has a daughter — what happened to her?" I asked.

"I did not know that; and I am as ignorant of her fate as I was, before you spoke of it, of her existence. But if Master Powers has taught you some of his skill, you will truly be of value."

"I shall do my best, sir." I was thinking of Faith. My friendship with her had been the closest I had ever come to having a sister. I looked at the Colonel. He prided himself on being concerned with the fate of a nation; and that little fraction of it which a child must be was too small to be worthy of his consideration. "I am most eager to be in Oxford, sir."

"If you truly wish to enter the lion's mouth, tomorrow I am sending a messenger there. You can travel as his servant. But once you are inside the walls of Oxford, you are alone. He will not know you — nor should you, I beg, know him! You are Colonel Cromwell's spy, not mine. I have respect for your master and shall forward any letter of yours that comes into my hands. But if anyone should ask me whether I have heard of you, I shall deny it. If Marshal Smith catches you and has you hanged, I shall be sorry, for you seem a likely lad. But no one will be able to rescue you."

I nodded. "I know, sir; we are but fleas to be cracked between two nails."

The Colonel laughed. "And in Oxford there will be plenty

of scratching. Because of the parliament the King has called, the town will be filled with strangers. Color your hair red and you can pass for an Irish boy."

"I was given the name of someone . . ." I began, but the Colonel held up his hand to interrupt me.

"I do not want to know who that person is. That is a matter between you and Colonel Cromwell. Whatever web he may be weaving, I care not to be caught up in it. I am the Commander for Parliament at Aylesbury, and I owe my allegiance to the Earl of Essex, who is my commander-in-chief."

Remembering my mission, as Major Ireton had described it to me, I bowed my head at the mentioning of Lord Essex's name, so that the Colonel could not see my face. But he was too absorbed in his own thoughts to notice.

"You are not well enough dressed to play the young gentleman in Oxford, since that town is filled with peacocks. My advice to you is to get some rags to wear. The man who will be taking you to Oxford is a poor carter. It will cause suspicion if his servant is better dressed than he is. He will have some clothes more suitable. Your own, you can leave with him; he is an honest fellow. As for your horse and saddle, if you come back to claim them, they will be yours again; but for the time being I shall make use of them."

"My horse is of little value, being past the age of use, sir." I was wondering if I could not somehow keep my clothes. I had not given thought to what disguise I should have in Oxford, if any; and although I recognized at once that the Colo-

nel's advice was sound, I wanted my friend Jack to see me
decently dressed, so that he would not need to be ashamed
of me.

These were silly thoughts, for in truth, Jack did not care
what I wore. Oh, but we who have inhabited the gutters and
back alleys of this world find it hard to give up the little
bits and pieces of glory that we collect on our way from
birth to grave.

The Colonel had called a young soldier into the room.
"Take this" — Colonel Mosley paused and looked at me —
"young gentleman to see Tom the carter."

"Thank you for your kindness, sir." I bowed and prepared
to follow the soldier.

"Tell Tom," the Colonel continued, speaking to the other
young man, "that I wish to see him at once." Now he turned
to me and a smile played on his lips. "If you say that I have
treated you well, you will be telling your master, Oliver
Cromwell, no lies. I have the greatest respect for him."

"And he for you, I am sure, for he called you his friend,"
I rejoined.

"Friend?" The Colonel wrinkled his brow. "To be sure
we are friends ... But remember, where you are going, you
may find none to bestow that title on. To spy on others is a
lonely occupation. My advice to you is to trust no one." The
Colonel grinned. "Call no one your friend in Oxford, not
even yourself."

"Aye, that be true, sir, that many a man is no friend to himself." I was thinking of my father. "Some even need no

enemy except the one they are given at birth. But I shall try to do nothing which can dishonor our cause, my master, or his friends." After this little speech, of which I was rather proud, I bowed once more; and this time, the Colonel wished me luck and gave me leave to go.

That Colonel Mosley did not trust me was abundantly clear — or was it Oliver Cromwell whom he did not trust? As I closed the door behind me, it struck me that Colonel Mosley was the kind of man who would not set his sails until he knew which wind was steady; and now there were so many that blew.

16
To Oxford

"Now no one would notice her," Tom the carter nodded towards his horse, a brown mare. "She is small, her tail is too short, and she has hairy legs. If you left her in a paddock with some other horses and a thief came to steal one, you can be sure, she would be the last beast he would pick. Yet she is a strong and steady animal. She is not showy and that is why she is best for us. Not to be seen — that is our profession."

"Have you been to Oxford many times as a messenger?" I asked. We were halfway there. A group of the King's cavalry had just passed us, but we had not even been noticed by them, though Tom had doffed his cap and bowed as they rode by.

"More often than I can count." Tom winked at me. "And I haven't done it for nothing, for though I love Parliament, there's no reason to give one's love away, as the wench said who married her master . . . Now when you be in Oxford, don't slink along the street like a cutpurse looking for a customer." The carter was fond of giving advice, a common failing, which does not make it easier to bear. "Act as if you were an apprentice who has just been sent on an errand by your master."

"You give me so much to remember that I shall be lucky if I recall the half of it," I grumbled.

"And doff your cap if you see any of the high and mighty. Never stare at them. If they be drunk, keep far away from them. They are hard enough to please when sober; and when they have drink taken then they are the devil to handle."

At that moment the cart almost tipped over. Tom had been too busy talking to notice a large stone and had driven the wheel of his cart onto it.

"There, you see, one must keep one's wits about one or one will come to grief." The carter liked to draw a moral from everything that happened to him. I am sure he believed that the rock had been placed in the middle of the road by Providence, and he took the opportunity to preach a homily over it. "Many a great load has been upset by a small stone," he said and sighed happily.

Any other time, Tom the carter might have amused me, but the news I had received in Aylesbury of the fate of my friend, Master Powers, did not incline me to laughter.

"Do you know," I asked, "what has happened to the innkeeper of the Unicorn?"

"Caught he was and papers aplenty in his house to prove his guilt." The carter's tone implied that he thought Master Powers a fool for having kept such evidence where it could

be so easily found. "He served good ale," he added grudg-
ingly.

"Will they hang him?" My voice shook.

"Probably." Tom was as cheerful as ever. "That is unless
he has some high connections. But they will make him talk
first."

In my mind I imagined Master Powers stretched on the
rack, though in truth, I had never seen one of those beds of
torture.

"On the other hand, they might not, for though the rack
has made liars tell the truth, it can make an honest man tell
lies as well."

"But hang him, they will," I whispered, and the fine, clear
winter sky seemed gray and dark to me.

"He will be food for ravens and crows, that is for sure,"
the carter nodded. "And that be a lesson for the rest of us
to be more careful."

Whatever made me look back at that moment, I do not
know; but I was thankful that I had. A lone rider was draw-
ing near us. Although I did not recognize him at once, something within me made me take caution. I stepped into the
ditch, so that I would be almost hidden from sight by the
heavily laden cart when he overtook us.

As the noise of the hoofs striking the road grew louder, I
quickly glanced up to see the rider. It was the Scottish
Laird!

"God's speed and blessings on you, sir!" I heard Tom cry
out. The carter had a way of speaking to strangers that

stamped him as a simpleton, and the Laird did not return his greeting.

"So I spoke the truth, after all, when I said he was a King's man," I thought. I watched him riding in the distance; he would be in Oxford long before we were. I almost expected to see the stolen pewter tankards dangling from his saddle, but he was no such fool. Whoever he had robbed of his horse must be a sorry man, for it was a fine animal.

"When we come to the gate say nothing," the carter warned. "Be as dumb as a dog; and if anyone should kick you, wag your tail!"

"Aye," I agreed.

Tom looked at me thoughtfully, then he let his hand glide along the wheel of the cart and smeared some of the dirt on my face. "A pity you don't have a snotty nose; that's as good a disguise as a lisp."

I smiled and pulled my woolen cap down over my head, but Tom pulled it back. "That won't do. Let them see you! If one of the soldiers pulls up your cap, he'll remember your face, if not till Doomsday, at least for a week."

Nothing that the carter had said or done during our trip from Aylesbury to Oxford had endeared him to me; yet he was often right and much of his advice stood me in good stead later.

"I have got two porkers, brought up like royal princesses, sir, on cream . . . Cabbages and leeks and some stone of onions. All for His Majesty, King Charles. God bless him, sir;

and may he drive all rebel dogs back to their kennels. I am but a plain countryman, sir, and I would —— "

"Talk my head off." The soldier lifted the tarpaulin and looked inside the cart. Satisfied, he flipped it back. "Now mind you, ask a fair price for your wares; or the King may pay you with a whipping instead of silver."

"Aye, sir," Tom bowed, "a striped back is but right payment for those who are greedy. I would gladly make a gift of everything, if it wasn't for the wife, sir, and the young ones at home."

"The poor bairns!" The soldier laughed. "I'll bet they are fed on cream as well, and that you have a bag of gold under your hearthstone."

"I am but a poor man!" Tom wailed. "By the sweat of my brow, as the Lord commanded, I earn my pennies."

"Like the fleas on a dog, you farmers suck our blood." The soldier waved his hand to tell us that we could pass through the gate of the city.

We crossed a meadow and soon would be on a street; we had already gone by a few houses. "Now our roads part," the carter murmured. "I shall be glad to share a jug with you in Aylesbury and you need not fear for your clothes. But should we meet again here, remember that we do not know each other."

I nodded and raised my hand in parting, then I walked more slowly to let Tom and his cart pass before me.

It was almost dark, but the streets were filled with people

and from one of the church towers came the sound of a bell. "You are back in Oxford, Oliver," I said to myself. "May the Lord send an angel to protect you, for you have need of it."

17
Master Drake

The snow and the cold proclaimed that it was a winter evening, but the crowds in the street reminded me more of a May Day fair. Some had had a drink too many, and some more than that. There were screaming and laughter: the kind of boisterous, hectic gaiety that foretells of bloody noses or worse to come.

I wanted to go first to the Unicorn. Even though I expected the tavern to be closed because of Master Powers's arrest, I hoped that his serving woman might be there and that she would be able to tell news of her master and his daughter, Faith. But long before I reached the inn, noise could be plainly heard coming from it. Two drunken soldiers with drawn swords tumbled out of the door just as I was about to open it. Though hardly able to stand upright, they deemed the street the proper place for settling some point of honor. Swearing and cursing loudly enough to be heard in both heaven and the other place they called upon, they lunged at each other. Quickly I turned and walked away; my visit to the Unicorn would have to wait.

Now I should have gone at once to the home of the man whom Colonel Cromwell had called "trustworthy." Yet so eager was I to see my friend Jack and tell him that I was back in Oxford, that I now set out in the direction of that house which he had pointed out to me belonged to his parents. As I walked along I smiled to myself, thinking of all the marvelous things I had to tell him; in my mind, I bathed in his admiration. It was not until I stood in front of the building that I remembered that his father was a King's man.

The house was not large. Lights shone from its windows. I saw a shadow and thought it might be Jack's. The idea that my friend was only a few yards away made me not only excited but hopeful as well, even though I dared not go to the door and knock.

I had just decided that I must go away, when a young maid came out of the house. I approached her, but she told me that she was in a hurry and had not the time for the likes of me.

"If I gave you a shilling would you have time then?" I asked.

"Let me see it," she demanded.

I dug the coin from my purse and held it between my thumb and forefinger.

"Give it to me!" she commanded; and the greed in her eyes told me that it was not often that she had a shilling she could call her own.

I let it fall into her hand; and she clenched it shut, as if it contained a treasure. "What do you want?" she asked.

"I want you to take a message to Jack . . . to Master John," I corrected myself and added, "it is important."

"To Master John!" she replied, amazed. "But he is not here. They sent him to his aunt in Cornwall."

"No!" I exclaimed unbelievingly.

"Oh yes!" The girl grinned. "It was a great disgrace. He kept bad company. I think he was with a band of robbers. One of them almost killed him; and if it hadn't been for the vicar's wife in Brill, they surely would have; but she chased the cutthroat away and saved Master John's life."

My daydreams had been too real to me. I could hardly grasp the meaning of her words.

"Are you one of them?" she asked.

"One of what?" I said, distracted.

"One of the robbers," she accused.

"Oh yes," I said bitterly, "I was their captain." I walked away leaving the girl to gape after me.

A board hanging from the upper story of the little house announced that it was inhabited by a tailor. "It takes nine tailors to make a man," I said to myself, while I thought how strange it was that this profession is so despised and yet all gentlemen place such value on their dress.

I knocked several times on the door before it was answered; and then it was opened only enough so that the girl, who had not unlatched it, could observe my face and ask my business.

"I wish to see Master Drake," I said, trying to sound as important as I could.

The girl appeared about to close the door again, when I whispered that I carried a message for him. "It is from a friend," I continued most earnestly, wondering how much I dared say. "East of here," I added.

"Wait," she finally uttered, as if to prove that she was not dumb, and then closed the door.

I do not know how long I waited, but it felt terribly long. It was very dark and bitterly cold. Several people passed in the street; I thought that they might be looking at me suspiciously. I was about to knock again, when the door was opened, but just wide enough to let me in.

The flickering light of the candle which the girl was carrying illuminated the little entrance hall. She was better dressed than a servant in such a modest house would be. "Come," she said softly and motioned towards a stairway.

On the landing of the second floor, she stopped in front of a door, on which she tapped gently. Without waiting for a response, she threw the door open and beckoned for me to enter; she did not follow me in.

The room was lit by two wax candles and a blazing fire. I could feel the warmth, though I was still standing in the doorway.

"Come closer." A tall, thin man, dressed in black, rose from his chair and held out his hand towards me. I noticed that he wore a heavy silver bracelet and that his linen cuffs were lined with lace. "My daughter said that you bring me news . . ." He hesitated, "Good news, I hope."

"Master Drake?" I asked almost timidly. He nodded, and I drew Colonel Cromwell's letter from inside my clothes. It was a bit wrinkled but the seal was still unbroken. "My name is Oliver Cutter."

Master Drake looked at the letter curiously, as if a message could be read on the outside of it.

"It carries no name because Major Ireton thought that if I should be captured, there was no reason to give the hounds more than a scent; a name would have shown them the way to the fox's den."

"How thoughtful of the Major." Master Drake smiled and pointed to a chair. He himself sat down once more before he broke the seal with a little knife and unfolded the letter. I watched his face as he read it. Although I did not know the wording, I was aware of its contents.

When he had finished, Master Drake scrutinized me slowly. "You are very young," he finally said.

"A fault that years will rectify," I answered, meeting his gaze.

"Aye, all who are old were young once . . . Though at times, this is hard to believe." The tailor grinned. "But not all who are young will live to be old."

"That is God's will — whether we die young or old." I could not make up my mind whether I liked Master Drake.

"Not a sparrow shall fall . . ." he continued good naturedly; but he grew more serious as he spoke. "It may be

God's will that the sparrow falls, but there is no reason to
tempt the hawk . . . I have respect for your Colonel. I met
him once, when I was in company of a friend of mine who
knows him well, a gentleman named Captain John Lilburne . . ."

I had heard of Captain Lilburne. He belonged to the Independents and was known for his sharp tongue. Once, when
the King had imprisoned him in the Tower of London, Colonel Cromwell had defended him.

"He has done great service for this friend, and I should
be ungrateful if I did not return it. But if I think that
you are a fool, I will have you sent away from Oxford,
whether Colonel Cromwell likes it or not, for I will not wear
the hempen neckband for your sake."

"I have thought, sir, while traveling here, that I may have
been sent on a fool's errand." Looking into the flames of the
fire, I tried to imagine what I would have thought of Oliver
Cutter had I been the tailor. "Still I shall do my best. I have
no more wish to provide food for ravens than you have,
sir."

Master Drake laughed. "Well said! Methinks we shall
work well together. Do you know a game called 'ducks and
drakes'?"

"You skip stones over the water and he whose stones skip
the most times wins. I played it on a pond near my home,
when I was a little child." I did not add that I had played it
only a few times and that with my father.

"Well, we are the stones, and the gentlemen, like your

Colonel Cromwell or our Earl of Essex, do the throwing. How many times will you and I skip across the water before we sink?"

"Ah, but a drake is not a stone; it can swim, sir."

Master Drake laughed. "We fit together. Your name if I heard rightly is Cutter. Well, a cutter cuts the cloth and a tailor sews it."

"And the tailor is master of the cutter, sir; and I shall serve you well."

"We shall turn this parliament of the King's inside out; and we shall know the hearts of each member." Master Drake looked thoughtfully into the fire. "There is another mention in the Bible of the sparrow. It is from the psalms. Number Twelve, if I remember correctly." The tailor rose and went over to the table on which the candles were standing. There a large book lay; leafing through it, he quickly found the page for which he was looking. "Yes, here it is: 'I watch and am as a sparrow alone upon the house-top.' Well, I have an attic room; it is cold, but otherwise, I think it will suit you. As for food, such as we eat, you will have and be welcome to it."

"I thank you, sir." I rose and bowed. I wanted to ask the tailor a thousand questions about Master Powers and his daughter, but I thought it unwise until I knew him better.

My room had one little gable window, which by chance faced the direction of the home of Jack's parents. In spite of the cold, I opened it and strained my eyes, hoping to see the house. But the building across the street obscured my view.

"Not that it matters," I told myself, "Jack is not there and you are alone." And strangely, this thought gave me a feeling of strength. "Oliver," I said, and smiled, "you cannot be a boy any longer. They have sent you on an errand for which you need to be a man."

18
Oliver the Spy

To those who do not know better, spying conjures up a world of secret meetings and nightly prowls as silent as the wings of the bat. My spying was not like that. Once the sun had set, I returned to my attic room; it was during the day I was busy. My work was to listen to gossip and to sift from the chaff those few grains of truth it contained.

Master Drake was not considered a great tailor, and few men of importance would have thought of requesting him to cut a coat; but he was well known for the quality of his repairs and — even more important — for doing them promptly. I took over, from his youngest apprentice, the delivery of these garments; and in his home I was treated according to my station, which was on a par with that of the little girl who scoured the pots and plucked the fowls. Unless we were alone, Master Drake never noticed me; and the apprentices thought me not worthy of their attention.

Within a few weeks there was hardly a house in Oxford I had not entered; and as for the colleges, I knew them as well as any scholar.

Soon servants treated me as one of their own; and since

a servant's time is his master's, he doesn't mind wasting it. Most were only too willing to talk; but those who best liked gossiping about their betters were not the most trustworthy. They were like poorly made mirrors which deform our features until we cannot recognize ourselves.

"He was a spy." The man who was speaking shook his head in wonder. "And I have been as close to him as I am right now to you. Many a glass of ale has he served me."

"Aye, it is hard to know who is honest and who is a scoundrel, these days," I agreed.

"But I had a feeling about him. A warning, you might say." The man-servant of the Royal cavalry captain to whom I had delivered a coat raised his finger in the air. "He was marked by God. Crook-backed he was, and that hump of his was the mark of the devil."

"He kept an inn, did you say?"

"Aye, the Unicorn was its name; and I will say for him his ale was good."

"Did he have a wife and will they hang her as well?" I asked, as though I had never heard of the owner of the Unicorn before.

The servant, who was a tall, gaunt man and looked more like a shadow than a human being, shook his head thoughtfully. "I wouldn't know ... I think he was a widower ... But he will be hanged! As soon as the Provost Marshal is finished with him, he will string him up." The man smiled happily as if the thought of Master Powers's death pleased him. "He had a lass, though. I remember that and *her* back was straight. Only the other day I heard someone tell my master that the Provost Marshal was looking for her."

"What would she know?" I asked too hastily and then said quickly, "That is if she is a mere lassie?"

The servant shrugged his shoulders. "You don't understand, boy. Though I might not have thought of it myself either. But crook-back is a hard nut to crack, and the Marshal thinks that she might be a nutcracker. There is five pounds to be earned by anyone who brings the lass to him. My master told me to keep my eyes open and I was to tell him if I did see her."

"And what does she look like?" I asked. My voice trembled and I hoped the captain's lackey would think it was eagerness for the money which made it quaver.

"She is but a lassie," he said, looking at me cunningly. "I can't remember what she looks like."

"Then you'll have a hard time finding her," I said with a laugh. "But if you do, remember to tell your master."

The servant grinned from ear to ear. "Aye, that for sure I shall. He owes me half a year's wages."

"My master will pay me mine with a stick, if I don't return to work," I said, while in my thoughts I cursed the fellow, for I felt certain that he did know what Faith looked like.

Luckily the tailor had no customers and I was able to see him as soon as I returned to his house. But before I could tell him what I had learned, he cheerfully announced that he had news which I would be glad to hear.

"Colonel Cromwell is no more," he exclaimed and then paused dramatically. "He is General Cromwell now!"

"General?" I repeated; I was still so occupied with thoughts of Faith that I was hardly listening to Master Drake.

"Are you not pleased?" The tailor was surprised and disappointed. "Oliver Cromwell is a Lieutenant General of Horse, and that will not harm you. Remember, when it rains on the master, it drips on his servants."

"It is good news, sir," I replied and smiled, though not joyously. "But I have something to tell you that is not pleasant."

When I had told Master Drake of my conversation with the captain's servant, he scowled. "I would outbid the Provost Marshal and happily pay ten pounds to have the girl here. Master Powers may be silent as an oyster, and so far as I know, he has told nothing. But if he saw his daughter stretched on the rack —— "

"They could not torture a child!" I almost shouted.

Master Drake threw up his hands in alarm. "Hush! Do not speak so loudly." Then he said sadly, "The Provost Marshal would do it out of love, Oliver. To torment others is his pleasure."

"We must find her," I pleaded, as if I thought that the tailor could draw little Faith out of his sleeve, had he wished.

"As I told you, she disappeared the night the Marshal's men arrested her father. There are those in Oxford who would have been only too glad to help her flee, if not for her sake then for their own ... I was not so closely acquainted with Master Powers, so I have little to fear even if the Marshal pried his mouth open," Master Drake explained.

"You said that his servant vanished, too?" I asked Drake.

"She was not from Oxford, I am told; and she may have taken Master Powers's daughter with her. They both may be far from here. Indeed, I think that that is most probable; still I cannot be sure of it."

"I remember her as a silent woman who kept her own counsel." To my despair, I could not even recall the features of the serving woman. "I will find Faith . . . if she is in Oxford," I added foolishly.

"You know, Oliver, you were not sent here to play the knight errant. The General would not be pleased if you were caught."

"The General . . ." For a moment I had forgotten my master's new rank. "No, he would be sorry." I smiled. "But Major Ireton would be furious."

"And right he would be, too." The tailor walked to the window. "I should be both sorry and frightened. Sorry for your sake and frightened for my own. I would fear that you could fit the hempen collar around my neck; and I have no wish to be raised above others at the end of a rope."

"Neither have I, so I shall be careful," I grinned with embarrassment, "for both our sakes."

"Do, Oliver, do!" Master Drake's tone was grave; but suddenly he laughed. "I have a coat to repair, which is promised for tomorrow. You can deliver it . . . You may hear something. The gentleman who owns it lives in one of the few houses in Oxford you have not been in yet."

"Whose coat is it?" I asked.

Master Drake spat out the name, "Provost Marshal Smith's!"

19

The Provost Marshal

Long before there were any colleges, Oxford Castle probably stood alone, a stone bastion in the midst of hovels. It belonged to times almost forgotten, and who built it, I have never heard tell. Now it was in disrepair and used only as a prison.

"You will find him in the tower there." The soldier on guard at the entrance pointed to the largest of the seven towers.

Fearfully, I looked around me, half-expecting to hear the screams of some tortured victim.

The soldier, noticing my reluctance to pass, laughed. "Beware, the Provost Marshal is not in the best of humors and he might have you roasted for dinner."

His gibe calmed me, and I walked on. The walls of the ancient tower were thick, and a damp smell met me as I entered. Several soldiers were standing in front of a small smoldering fire, trying to warm themselves by its feeble embers.

"What do you want?" one of them asked gruffly.

"I have come to deliver the Provost Marshal's coat, which my master has repaired," I said courteously and bowed.

An old soldier was ordered to accompany me. My guide led me to a narrow passage and up a flight of stairs, which, though they were of stone, had steps so worn by use that they sloped towards the middle. The only light came from a slit halfway up the wall.

"Here, boy." The stairs continued, but the soldier stopped before a door in the inner wall and knocked on it.

The room I now entered was larger than the one below. The fireplace was grander and must have had a better draft, for there was a goodish blaze in it.

"This boy says he has a coat of yours, sir." The old soldier bowed towards a figure seated in a chair before the fire, and then retired, closing the door behind him.

"Bring it here, boy. The last time your master seemed to have nothing but thumbs when he did the sewing. I might as well have had my own servant do it." His voice was thin, like an old woman's.

Warily, I stepped forward. I would not have been in the least surprised had the Provost Marshal had the face of a monster. As I handed him the coat, he looked up at me. He had finely chiseled features, framed by an abundance of brown locks that curled to his shoulders. Only his lips marred his visage; they were thin and made his mouth appear like a slit in his face.

"Are you afraid of me, boy?" The Marshal smiled. "I fear that I have gotten too much of a reputation lately." With deft fingers, he examined the place where the coat had been repaired, nodding in approval of what he found. "Mary!" he called loudly.

Silently a serving woman entered, and the Provost Marshal held out his coat to her. She took it; and without either of them having said a word, she disappeared as quietly as she had come.

"What do they say of me in the town?" the Marshal demanded and looked at me steadily with small, dark brown eyes. "Come, speak up, boy!"

"They say that you make the dead speak and make living men tremble." I kept my gaze as steady as his.

"The hangman and I do our jobs well, but we get little thanks for it." The Provost Marshal glanced into the fire. "If a tailor cuts a fine coat, he is deemed a master. If I make a rebel speak, who would otherwise have kept his mouth closed, I am thought to be a fiend . . . But surely," the man smiled and looked at me again, "the Lord God keeps the fires of hell burning; and no one blames him for having Satan as his servant."

I nodded in agreement, though I thought to myself, "King Charles is not God."

"It seems that certain gentlemen of the King's parliament have complained of me," the Provost Marshal remarked bitterly. "I could tell His Majesty that he will get no more out of this parliament than the one at Westminster. Men are like dogs: they can best be ruled by the whip."

"I am but a boy, sir, and know little of this," I ventured when the silence seemed to have lasted too long.

"Of the whip?" He smiled unpleasantly. "I thought all apprentices have their backs kissed by it."

"I meant, sir, that I am too young to know how best the King should govern."

"You are a rarity." The Provost Marshal laughed. "It seems to me that here in England even the babes at their mothers' breasts will stop suckling long enough to preach a homily for His Majesty's edification."

"It is not for me, sir, to tell my betters what to do." I tried to make my voice as humble as my words.

"You are probably a liar." The Marshal grinned and looked as friendly as a weasel in the henhouse. "When you get home to your peers, I am sure that in your garret you plan rebellion, like the apprentices of London. But remember here the King still rules and if there are not enough gallows, we can hang you from the trees."

"Aye, I have no wish to be an apple that will hang from those branches. But surely, it is not from the likes of me that there have been any complaints against a man as mighty as you are, sir?"

"As mighty as I am," the Marshal repeated my words slowly as if to taste them, then finding that they agreed with his palate, he smiled. "Aye, within these walls, I am master. But there are those fine gentlemen who are too sensitive to drown a puppy themselves, and therefore, ask their gamekeeper to do it. Yet they do not like him for it and call him a brute for obeying the orders that they themselves have given." The Provost Marshal sniffed with anger. "If I have made crook-back a little more twisted than he was, what difference does it make? When I hang him, I will put a weight at his feet and straighten him out."

"He is a traitor!" I exclaimed, hoping thereby to show my loyalty to the King.

"Did you know him? Speak up, boy." The Provost Marshal jumped up from his chair.

For a moment, I thought of pretending that I did not know who crook-back was; but one glance at the Provost Marshal made me think better of it. "There is much talk about him, sir. They say that he is in league with the devil." I lowered my voice almost to a whisper, as if the thought of what I was about to tell terrified me. "They say Master Powers can change himself into the shape of a dog, and can change others into toads and rats, if it pleases him."

" 'They' are a fool's tongue." The Provost Marshal seated himself again and grinned. "If crook-back could change me into a toad, he would have ... He has a daughter about your age," he said as his gaze sought mine. "You are a fine looking lad; I am sure you know every lass in Oxford."

While trying to show my gratitude for the compliment by smiling, I shook my head. "I have never been at his inn, sir. He would not allow apprentices there."

"In that crook-back showed some sense; for of all the

vermin, apprentices are the hardest to get rid of. But there is a pretty purse for anyone who can tell me where crook-back's daughter is. Remember that, boy, if you ever hear of a girl whose name is Faith Powers."

"I shall, sir," I said and bowed.

"Now be off with you. I shall settle with your master myself." The Provost Marshal was known for never paying his debts.

I closed the door behind me and walked slowly down the uneven steps, letting my hand glide over the damp wall.

"Well, did he eat you?" The old soldier who had been my guide grinned. "But if he tipped you, I will give you a sovereign."

"Not as much as a farthing," I replied, which made all the soldiers around the poor little fire laugh.

"And now you and your master have been paid equally well," the old man said.

"If all the ships that sailed the sea were as tight as the Provost Marshal, none would ever sink," another proclaimed.

Just as I was about to step across the threshold of the tower, a soldier grabbed my arm, and demanded, "Did he ask you about crook-back's daughter?"

"Aye," I answered. "And he told me to come and see him if I should hear of her."

"Now don't be a fool, boy. Tell me where she is, and if I catch her, I'll give you a sovereign, at least!"

"For sure, I shall!" I shouted, for he was hurting my arm. All the soldiers laughed and he let me go.

As I walked across the courtyard of the castle, I wondered whether the fiends in hell laughed when they tortured the souls condemned to that place.

20

The Two Ravens

On my way back to Master Drake's house, I thought about what I had learned from my visit to Oxford Castle. That the Provost Marshal took the complaints against his reign in that prison seriously gave good reason for rejoicing. He would hardly have talked as he had, to someone as humble as a tailor's boy, had he not felt himself hard pressed. It is when a master tries to justify himself to a servant that you know his peers will no longer listen to him. But was it not this very news which explained his search for Faith? If he could use her to make Master Powers confess, he would have a pretty story to tell royal ears. It was a desperate venture: his cruelty had to bear sweet fruits in order to be forgiven. If Faith was still in Oxford, I would have to find her before the Marshal's men did. It was a race, and I was far from certain that I would win.

So lost was I in my thoughts, that I paid little attention to where I was going. Suddenly I became aware that someone was keeping pace with me. I turned to see who it was. A poor woman, dressed in a ragged cloak with a hood that hid her face was walking beside me.

"Tonight at the Two Ravens," she whispered. "The door at the rear will be unbarred."

"Who sent you?" I asked.

"It is not far from the castle," the woman replied as if that were an answer to my question.

"Who sent you?" I repeated my demand; but the woman walked on without taking any further notice of me, like a person in a dream.

For a moment I thought of running after her; but there were so many people in the street that soon she was lost among the other passers-by.

Had she spoken to me at all? Wasn't it something I had imagined? "The Two Ravens," I thought. "It sounds like the name of a tavern; and yet there is not an ale house in all of Oxford that I have not been in." These had been my favorite hunting grounds for gathering news.

"Are you moonstruck?" It was one of Master Drake's apprentices.

Dazed, I looked around me. I was standing right in front of the tailor's house.

"Do you know of a tavern called 'The Two Ravens'?" I asked.

"I never heard of it." The apprentice grinned. "But then I seldom have two pennies to rub together."

"Aye, ours is a hard life," I said and waved to him as I walked away.

I was determined to try to find the tavern the woman had spoken of. What if it wasn't anywhere and no one else had ever heard of it? Well, then I had gone mad. The woman had been a specter and I was moonstruck.

As I neared Oxford Castle, the dwellings became more dilapidated. This was one of the poorest quarters of the city. An hour before, I had hardly noticed one miserable shelter from the next; but now each attracted my attention, for among them I must find a tavern.

A child came out of one of the hovels and began to follow me. He was begging. If any of the mighty had bothered to look at me as I walked on High Street or St. Aldates, they would have thought, "There goes a poor boy." But here I belonged to the rich. Worn though it was, I had a warm jacket; and there were boots on my feet, no matter that they were clumsily cut. It was winter and this child's rags barely covered his little body and he was barefooted. "I have been as poor as that, too," I thought. When my father and I went "a-soldiering" my feet had been bare.

"Would you know where 'The Two Ravens' is?" I asked.

The boy's head bobbed up and down, and eagerly he said that he would lead me there, which was fortunate, for I would not have found it otherwise. It had no sign to show that there was a tavern within; it was merely an old house among many others.

I gave the boy a penny. I would have liked to give him more, but I was afraid he would brag to his friends about his luck, and then I would have a pack of children at my heels.

On one side the house was leaning against its neighbor; on the other there was an alley. I took a few steps down this narrow passageway. From the rear the building looked even more as if the next good wind might blow it down. It was three stories high, but halfway up, the wall bulged like a woman with child. Below this enormous curve was a door. "That is the one the woman promised would be unbarred," I thought. A low fence ran round a bit of land, which probably had once been a garden, but now was filled with rubbish.

The Two Ravens was obviously one of those ale houses which had sprung up in Oxford since the King had made his headquarters here. Like the drainage in the streets, they served a purpose; but they were unlawful and every once in a while the Provost Marshal closed them. The owners of these taverns were like the birds that flock around a battlefield, thinking it a table decked for them. "Its name describes it well," I thought, "since ravens are carrion birds."

Now if I had been sensible, I should have returned to Master Drake and told him of my adventures. Certainly, I should not have gone inside the ale house, but my curiosity was greater than my usual caution.

If the tavern presented a sorry visage to the world, it was even less inviting once you were inside. Whether the floor was of flagstone or earth, I could not judge, so long had it been since it was swept. Cobwebs decorated the beams and flyspecks the walls. The furnishings looked as if they had been fashioned with an axe and polished with the same tool. The customers fitted the benches on which they were sitting. I had never seen a more rough-looking lot. "Gallows food," I thought and was relieved to find a stool in a distant corner.

"And what would you want, me love?" The woman smiled at me. Her two front teeth were missing. As she had walked towards me, I had noticed that her bare feet were as dirty as the floor she trod upon. I looked closely at her face. She was not the same woman who had spoken to me in the street. The other one had been taller.

The ale was poor, and had it been a month or two hence, I would not have been surprised to find a tadpole in it. The room was warm, though. A good fire blazed on the hearth. All conversation had ceased when I entered. I wondered who they thought I was; and then decided that they might think me one of the Provost Marshal's spies.

No one spoke to me, while I sat and tried to sip that foul drink. Finally I paid my reckoning, though I left most of what I had paid for untouched.

I stepped into the street and found the little beggar waiting for me. Over and over again, he told me how hungry he was, dancing first on one side of me and then on the other. At last, I gave him a shilling; and I cursed myself as soon as I had done it. The boy did not look like a fool, who would not know that apprentices did not have shillings to throw about.

He grinned and interlaced his many thanks with more than half a dozen "sirs."

21

An Irish Chieftain and the Scottish Laird

If I had not been afraid of attracting attention, I might have run, at least part of the way, from the Two Ravens back to Master Drake's. I was as filled with news as the baskets of a farmer traveling to town are with cabbages, and, like the farmer, I was most eager to be rid of my wares. It did not even occur to me that the tailor might not be at home; my only worry was that he would have a customer and I should have to wait to see him. The silence that greeted my first gentle tapping on his door did not discourage me; I merely knocked louder.

"My father has gone out." It was Master Drake's daughter. He was a widower and had two children: a son who was still a child and this girl. She could move as silently as a cat. I had not heard her, although she must have followed me up the stairs. "Is it anything important?" she asked.

"No, miss, it is nothing." I smiled at the girl. She was the only member of the household who I suspected might know that more than tailoring was going on within its walls. "I only wanted to tell the master that I received no payment for the coat I delivered."

"That will not surprise my father." The girl smiled as well. "That particular customer of his has never been known to pay."

I marveled that the girl had chosen deliberately to tell me that she knew to whom I had brought a jacket that morning. "Will the master be back late?" I asked.

"I don't know. My father does not tell me everything."

"Secrets when told are secrets no longer." I tried to sound gay. Without knowing why, I mistrusted the girl.

"That is true." The expression on her face was very serious. "They say secrets are sweet, but I think that too many of them are a bitter burden." She turned her back on me and walked down the stairs.

As I watched her go, I decided that I must tell her father of our conversation. If she had guessed too much and was told too little, she could be a danger to us all. "How wretched it is to be a spy," I thought. Suspicion was becoming part of my nature. How happy I would have been to be Cromwell's boy again: to ride my mare and live in Huntingdon.

"The girl is lonely," I told myself. "She has no one to talk to." The woman who cooked for Master Drake was surly and had a rough tongue.

I passed through the entrance hall and heard noise coming from the room where the apprentices worked. They were having a great argument, which only the return of Master Drake would settle.

The tailor's house was near the inner walls of the city. As I made my way to Christ Church, which was now the King's residence, I tried to imagine what Oxford had looked like in time of peace. Now there were soldiers everywhere instead of students. "I should like to be a student," I thought, and I pictured myself living in one of the beautiful colleges. "I would learn Latin and Greek." It was only a dream, and yet even to play with such an idea only a year ago would have been impossible for me. But the pleasure of remembering the boy I had been compared to the youth I had become was suddenly overcast by a memory of the blacksmith and his wife. That good man and woman had been kind to me when I had been as poor as the child who led me to the Two Ravens; and I had not bothered to visit them, though for months I had lived but a few miles away in Huntingdon. My promise to bring the blacksmith's wife a gift from London had been forgotten long before I had even reached that great city.

"Get out of the way, boy!"

So deep had I been in thought that I did not notice the approach of a group of cavaliers much the worse for drink. I stepped aside just in time and doffed my cap.

With a haughty glance in my direction and a small nod to acknowledge my bare head, one of them nearly knocked me down, while the others tripped by.

I smiled to myself and wondered what they would have thought had they known they had passed so close to a spy for the "Roundheads."

"They are as arrogant as the cock in the henyard." The young man who seemed to be speaking to himself wore a cape of strange cut over his shoulders. "On the battlefield I'll wager they'll teach lessons to the deer."

"Some are courageous enough," I said. "But here they are idle, for there is nothing to do but down ale."

"Nothing to do!" He was obviously a young man so angry that the buttons on his coat might burst any minute from having to contain so much wrath. "Here the greatest battle is fought! The siege of the royal ear! Tell King Charles what he wants to hear and you can become a general." Then with a sneer, he added, "Or Lord President of Munster!"

I wanted to ask him what it meant to be Lord President of Munster but I didn't dare. "Are you a member of parliament?" I inquired timidly.

The young man laughed. "One of the King's sheep. No, I am not." He was staring at his feet, which were encased in a fine pair of boots.

Hoping to keep him in conversation I mumbled, "Do not all kings like flattery?"

"That is the weakness of all men who have power; and yet it is the surest way of losing it," he replied good-naturedly.

"You are right . . ." I muttered.

He glanced down at me as if he had suddenly become aware to whom he was speaking and this realization left him much surprised. "I am Lord Inchiquin, and my name is O'Brien. A better name in Ireland it would be hard for the

King to find; but he favors Lord Antrim. And I might as well have saved myself the trouble of coming to Oxford."

"I am sorry, sir." This news might be of interest to General Cromwell, and I tried to think of something to say which would gain me more information. "And he is to be Lord President of . . . of . . ."

"Munster!" the young man exclaimed and then shrugged his shoulders. "It is of no consequence to you — you would not even know where Munster is." He laughed. "I think I must be going mad. I shall be talking to my shadow next." He drew from his purse a shilling and handed it to me. "There, and remember whatever you say about the Irish, you cannot complain that they are mean."

"I never shall, sir." I bowed, and the young nobleman would have walked on, if another group of drunken soldiers had not come at that very moment and forced us both to step aside.

There were about a dozen of them in that state when all were convinced that God gave them voices to sing. The young Irish Lord looked at me and winked; then he laughed. But I turned pale. The man leading the revelers was the Scottish Laird who had stolen the pewter from the inn-keeper at Ampthill. For a moment our eyes met.

The Scot's eyebrows rose in surprise, and he made a little bow towards me, which the Irish nobleman thought was courtesy to him and he returned it.

"Tomorrow they will complain that someone has stolen

the silver out of their purses, for they won't be able to recall how they spent it." The young Irishman shook his head, nodded, and walked on.

"God's blessing on you, sir!" I called to his back, while I fervently prayed that he was right, that the Scot would forget that he had seen me. But he had been the least drunk of the soldiers, and he had recognized me. Would he not wonder what I was doing in Oxford clothed as a poor apprentice? When last he had seen me, I had been well dressed, with money in my purse to buy him ale.

22

Master Drake's Daughter

Master Drake's daughter met me at the door, when I returned to her father's house, and I suspected that she had been waiting for me.

"Has the master come back?" I asked. It was a foolish question, for the noise coming from workroom told me that the cat was still away.

"No, I thought you might have seen him." The girl looked at me so intently that I turned away, as if I had committted some crime in not having searched the town for her father.

"He will be back soon," I mumbled as I mounted the stairs. To my surprise the girl followed me. As I put my hand on the latch of the door, which led to a narrow corridor at the end of which were the ladderlike stairs to my attic, she touched my shoulder.

"Why don't you go away?" she demanded.

"Go away?" I repeated. "Why do you want me to go away?"

"Because some day the Marshal's men might come and take

my father, and it will be the likes of you who have caused it." Her voice rose. "And what will become of me and my brother?"

The landing was no place for an argument. "Come," I said; taking her by the arm, I led her to Master Drake's room. "I shall be going away soon," I assured her, when I had closed the door behind us.

"It doesn't matter." There were tears in the girl's eyes. "Somebody else will come, and there will be the same light tapping on the door when all honest men are abed . . . And nothing will he tell me . . . As if I were a child."

"There are things that it is better not to know." In the wild hope of seeing the tailor, I walked to the window and looked down; but the street was empty.

"It is always better to know," the girl protested. "Every time my father leaves the house, I wonder if he will return. And when customers call, I look at them carefully to try to guess whether they be good men or thieves and robbers."

"Thieves and robbers!" I was amazed and relieved that the girl had so misjudged her father.

"I would rather be poor than have anything to do with the likes of . . . of them." She pushed a lock of hair away from her face. I knew that what she had wanted to say had been *you,* not *them.* It was obvious that Master Drake had never told his children of his true beliefs; and the remarks he had made to convince his customers of his loyalty to the King had deceived his household as well.

"Your father is as honest as any man in Oxford!" I exclaimed.

A forlorn smile passed over the girl's face. She wanted to believe me. "The cook says that you do little work for your keep; and the little lassie who helps her says you spend all night writing."

"I am copying texts from the Bible to teach myself a fair hand," I lied. "But if the cook wags her tongue too much, she can bring trouble to her master. I shall talk with him and tell him of your fears. But I can tell you that Master Drake has done nothing dishonest for which you need feel shame."

"I do believe you." The tailor's daughter sighed. "But only now ... When night comes and I am lying in my bed, dreadful dreams come to me and then my fears will return."

"Your father will laugh when I tell him that you think he is a thief," I said to the girl in parting, and tried to laugh myself. But she looked back at me with an expression of sadness; and I was reminded that Master Drake, though kind, always treated his children in a strange and distant manner.

As I climbed the stairs to my attic room, I tried to imagine what it would be like to be a child of the tailor. I had never seen him show any sign of affection to either his daughter or his son; and yet his eyes could gleam with passion when he spoke of his ideals and of his friend Captain Lilburne. Master Drake's children must have missed their mother terribly. She had died in childbirth. "It was two years after the King sent the Parliament packing for the first time," the tailor had explained to me. Like Ezra, he hated King Charles and hoped for a time when there would be no kings. It was from his lips that I first heard the word "republic."

I glanced around the little room which for almost a month had been my home. I would not miss it when I left — and leave I would have to soon. I had not liked what the tailor's daughter had told me of the gossiping of the cook and the little scullery maid. They were foolish creatures, both of them; and because of that all the more dangerous.

From beneath the straw of my bed, I drew out some sheets of paper that had been written upon. I had sent only one report to Cromwell. These were attempts which had not satisfied me. I picked up a page and read: "For his Excellency Oliver Cromwell, Colonel of the Eastern Division." I had been very proud of that beginning; it was like the ones I had seen on letters to the General and Major Whalley. But a few lines farther down, a large ink blot revealed why this particular sheet had been abandoned and the remainder of the paper used for practicing. "Your most obedient servant..." "I rest, your obedient servant..." and finally, "Your servant" told that I had been in some doubt about the proper closing.

I took these pages down to Master Drake's room, where a fire was burning, and fed them to the flames. As I watched them flare up and then become ashes, I wondered whether the General had received my letter and what he had thought of it. Master Drake had had it smuggled to Aylesbury. Unless there had been a mishap, it must be in Ely by now. Because I had no seal, I had put two hairs in the wax, so that if it were tampered with Cromwell would be able to see it.

23

Appointment in the Night

One of the town clocks struck eight. I decided that I could wait no longer for the tailor to come home.

The night was clear and starlit. I walked faster and faster. It was as if the back door of the inn, which I had been promised would be left unbarred, drew me like a lodestone.

The house looked bigger and more mysterious in the darkness. Now, for the first time, I thought that something evil could be waiting for me inside: some great beast of the night which would pounce upon me the moment I stepped across the threshold. I told myself that these were childish fears, but reason rules best when one is seated in front of a warm fire.

A gust of wind blew against my face. The shutters of the tavern were closed, but on the second floor of the house a window was dimly lit.

The moon was rising. It was a new moon. The silver sickle glowed sharply just above the chimney. There was no point in waiting; yet I tarried, trying to bring my fears to heel. I looked in every direction; someone else might be watching the inn.

Finally, keeping as much in the shadows as I could, I crossed the street and walked down the narrow, dark passage that ran alongside the tavern. No lights shone from any of the windows in the back of the house, but the shutters may all have been closed.

There was the door. It looked much like any other door. I lifted the latch and was prepared to push, but it opened easily and silently. I decided to leave it ajar, in order to take advantage of the bit of starlight that came through the opening.

I was in a hall. I could hear noise coming from the kitchen and the tavern beyond it. These sounds calmed me because they were not ghostlike.

There were two inner doors: one obviously led to the kitchen. I opened the other and peered into pitch darkness. Half-expecting to fall into some bottomless pit, I stepped inside. I held out my arms and touched the opposite wall. I thought that I had entered a closet and was about to return to the hall, when that, too, became totally black. Someone — or maybe only the wind — had closed the outside door.

I stood perfectly still, listening; but the loudest noise I could hear was the beating of my own heart. Clinging to the wall, I turned and took a step forward. I lifted my feet slowly as if I were walking in a bog. My foot touched something; I knelt down. It was the bottom tread of a flight of stairs.

I started to climb, first one step and then the next. I heard something. I held my breath. All houses are filled with noises; more than human beings make their homes under their roofs — mice and rats are burrowing in their walls.

Something touched my ankle, softly, like a ghostly hand. I shuddered and bent down. I felt a warm, furry coat.

The cat began to purr and I picked it up. It was used to being petted and snuggled into my arms. When I reached the landing, I saw a dim line of light beneath a door.

I stroked the cat, and it acknowledged my caress by purring even louder. "Should I knock on the door or just open it?" I whispered.

The cat had no opinion upon the matter. I found the latch, lifted it, and peeped inside. The first thing I saw was the fire blazing on the hearth. Coming from the darkness, the light seemed very bright. On the mantelpiece were two tallow candles. Silently I opened the door a little more and stole into the room. At first, I thought it was empty, and I was both disappointed and relieved. But it was larger than I had supposed; and at the far end, beside a window, someone was standing. His back was towards me, and he was looking intently down into the street below.

Quietly I closed the door behind me. What a warm and lovely room it was! In one corner was a bed and in the middle a table. The remnants of a dinner were still on it. The cat meowed loudly and wiggled in my arms; it had spied bits of meat on one of the plates.

With a start, the figure at the window turned around; then he stood still and grinned. "Why don't you put your friend down, Oliver, so that I can greet you properly?"

"Jack!" I shouted and the cat dropped to the floor, as I ran to embrace my friend. "But you are in Cornwall!" I exclaimed. "The maid in your father's house told me so."

"Are you going to trust her tongue or your own eyes?" Jack, still laughing, grasped my shoulders. "You have grown both widthwise and upwards."

"And so have you," I said and tried to hide my regret, for though I had grown, the vain hope that Jack and I would now be the same size was gone. He had become a man.

"And rich as Croesus, you are too." He studied me from head to toe, and back up again. "Though you don't look it."

"Rich?" I repeated with surprise.

"Do poor people usually give a shilling to every urchin from whom they ask directions?"

"No," I smiled happily. "So he was one of your spies. I gave him a shilling because he reminded me of myself. . . . Do you remember what I looked like when we first met at Worcester?"

"I do," Jack replied thoughtfully. "I recall you had a snotty nose."

"I did not!" I protested indignantly.

"Oh yes," Jack nodded. "You had a runny nose and a dirty face; and you were about this height." He bent down and held out his hand about two feet above the ground; then he burst out laughing. "But I am glad . . . Oh God, I am glad to see you!"

24

The Cause of Parliament

When finally something happens which you have dreamed about a hundred times, it rarely takes place as you have imagined it. Not you, but fate decides the time and circumstances. I had daydreamed of meeting Jack wearing my best clothes, with a sword at my side, and preferably riding a fine horse. In my fantasies, he admired me and I was, at last, his equal.

But that was not to be. Jack was attired in a short coat of velvet and a lace collar, while I resembled any apprentice you might see in the streets of Oxford running an errand for his master. This might not have mattered, if there had not been other differences as well. It seemed to me that Jack had changed. His laughter was not as merry as it used to be; and though he still spoke softly, his voice had an edge of sharpness. He was fervently for Parliament, and spoke of King Charles with a venom and contempt that I had never heard him express before. He reminded me of Major Ireton; and like the Major, he could at times appear cruel rather than just.

Childishly, I had hoped to tell him how I had become a messenger for a general, and perhaps even boast of how I was called Cromwell's boy, back in Huntingdon. But Jack seemed hardly interested in hearing of my advancement, though he asked a thousand questions about my master and the state of the army. Most of his queries I could not answer to his satisfaction — at least, so I felt.

To be just to him, he spoke little of himself as well. He did not tell of high deeds he had done in Cornwall or even explain what he was doing now in Oxford. I should not have minded had he bragged a little. He was my only friend; and I thirsted for an intimacy which he seemed unable — or worse, unwilling — to give me.

After our first embrace and a few more jesting words, we sat down in front of the fire; and I felt much like some trusted sergeant who was speaking to his lieutenant. The cat, which had so scared me on the stairs, had returned to my lap; and I stroked it until it purred with pleasure.

"There are only two sides now, Oliver; and every man in England will have to make up his mind which he belongs to. But ours is a swift river and the King's a swampy bog."

I glanced at my friend. He looked so earnest; yet I could not help saying, "River or bog, Jack, you can drown in either."

"Aye," Jack smiled. "We play for high stakes. The King calls us traitors and would cut off our heads, if he could."

"And sometimes he can. Is not Master Powers in his claws?"

"There is no great cause which has not had its martyrs."
Jack looked at me solemnly; and I turned my head away
because I suddenly felt ashamed, for I knew at that moment
that I did not want to be a martyr, even for the cause of
Parliament.

"Is Faith to be a martyr, too?" I demanded, and to my
surprise my voice sounded angry.

"I hope not," Jack replied. "You were fond of the girl,
were you not?"

"Aye," I answered. I was at the point of adding, "I was,"
when I decided to say instead, "I am fond of her!"

"If the cause of Parliament needed it, I should gladly give
up my life." The expression on Jack's face was grave. "Our
cause is the cause of justice, and that is more important than
the life of a child."

"You have a sister, whom you once told me that you
were fond of. She is younger than you — about the age of
Faith. What if it were her life that was in danger?"

While I spoke Jack scowled, but now he suddenly smiled.
"But Faith is safe, and the Provost Marshal's men cannot
catch her."

"Where is she?" I asked and squeezed the cat so hard that
it meowed and leapt from my lap.

"We cannot afford to let kindness determine our actions,
if they, in turn, stand in the way of the triumph of justice.
We must — "

"Where is she?" I cried, interrupting Jack's philosophizing. "Do you know that the Provost Marshal has offered a

reward to anyone who will tell him where she is to be found?"

"No!" Jack was shamefaced. "I knew that he was looking for her, but not that he had baited his hook with gold."

"Well, he has," I said and explained to Jack how I had first heard of the reward from a servant of one of Master Drake's customers. Then I told him of my own meeting with Provost Marshal Smith.

"You are not easily frightened, are you?" For the first time there was a note of admiration in Jack's voice.

I shook my head, "You are wrong." The cat had jumped back into my lap and I started petting it again. "Sometimes at night, when I am lying in bed, I imagine what might happen to me, and I grow so cold with fear that I shiver."

"Faith is safely hidden with some friends of Parliament here in Oxford." Jack pulled the sleeves of his jacket down, and I realized that he had outgrown it.

"I met someone, by chance, today, Jack . . ." And I told my friend about the Scottish Laird and how convinced I was that he had recognized me. "I think it is best that I leave Oxford, if not for my own sake then for Master Drake's. My faith in my own courage is not great enough to persuade me that I would remain silent on the rack." I grinned, for at that moment I felt certain that I would not fall into the hands of the Provost Marshal. "Would it not be best if the girl went with me?"

"Aye, it would be better for all of us, if she were not here." Jack frowned. "But to get her through the gates will not be easy, especially if there is a price on her head."

"Master Drake will see to that!" I exclaimed. "It is he who smuggles my letters out; and he is in constant contact with the Parliamentary garrison in Aylesbury."

"I should like to meet Master Drake," Jack said and looked at me questioningly.

"I shall tell him," I replied. "But he is not the kind of man who willingly climbs out on branches which he thinks will not carry him."

"We are both for Parliament," Jack said confidently, as if he were speaking a secret password. Living in territory held by King Charles, he had little knowledge of the factions that existed within Parliament, or of the quarreling and suspicion that were rife in our army.

"Aye," I laughed, "but that you both support Parliament does not mean that you will agree on much else."

"Whom does Master Drake follow?"

I shrugged my shoulders. "I am not certain. There is no reason for me to know what does not concern me, but the name of Captain Lilburne is often on his tongue." I turned away from Jack, as if I feared that by seeing my face he could read my thoughts. I was wondering what he would say if he knew of the instructions I had received from Major Ireton.

"I have heard of John Lilburne," Jack remarked thoughtfully. "I hope I did not offend you by not revealing where Faith is hidden."

"I was eager enough to know," I admitted, "but it is best that I don't. What I do not know, the Provost Marshal can never convince me to tell."

"The Marshal has lost the King many a friend," Jack said lightheartedly. "They hold the dark deeds which he performs in Oxford Castle against King Charles, as if he himself had done them."

"And so they should!" I replied almost angrily, for I felt that by his jesting tone Jack had shown once more that he did not wish to be intimate with me.

"I sometimes think that the Provost Marshal does more for our cause than all the preachers of London. If the King's parliament fails, it will be partly thanks to him."

"I can well do without his help, and so I believe could his prisoners. Although what you say may be true ... His cruelty serves our cause well," I muttered bitterly. I was thinking of Master Powers lying in a dungeon, his limbs broken by the rack.

Jack looked into the fire; now he was no longer smiling. "It does not matter how we win, whether it be by our own valor or the cowardice of the cavaliers. Our cause is just, and what is important is that victory be ours. I tell you, Oliver, our cleverness would be of no avail if we could not count on the King's foolishness. If Charles listened to his Secretary of State, Sir Edward Nicholas, or to Edward Hyde, and allowed Prince Rupert to command the army, we would have little hope of victory. But King Charles trusts Lord Digby above everyone else, and with such an adviser next to the royal ear, we are bound to win."

While Jack was speaking, the face of the tailor's daughter, when she was telling me that she suspected her father of being a thief, came into my mind. For a moment I thought of telling Jack about her; but then I dismissed the idea. "He would not be interested," I said to myself silently. He who cared so little for Faith, whom he knew, would not wish to hear about a stranger's daughter. "You have not told me how Faith fares," I said aloud.

Jack looked surprised. "She is well taken care of," he replied.

I put the cat down and stood up. "You have changed," I said sadly.

"We cannot stay children forever." Jack smiled. "You too have changed. I will wager that even Ezra is not the same boy that we knew."

I nodded as if I agreed. One of the things that I had most looked forward to telling Jack was of my meeting with Ezra. Now I no longer wanted to talk of it. I felt very tired, as if nothing mattered anymore.

"Can Faith be ready when I send word for her?" I asked.

"She has nothing to pack," Jack said, but then he must have realized how flippant this sounded, for he added quickly, "She is a brave little lass."

"A brave little lass," I repeated Jack's words and then, grinning, I said, "and we are brave lads, too." I walked to the window and looked down in the street. "Do you remember William, Ezra's lieutenant . . . the boy who, even when he was dying, wanted to believe that Lord Essex was his father?"

"Poor fool." Jack's voice was as soft as it used to be.

"When we die with the word 'Parliament' on our lips, won't we be poor fools, too?" Hearing my own words, I was surprised; it was as if a stranger within me had spoken.

"No!" Jack exclaimed and I turned to look at him. "His lie was vanity! Our sacrifice is made for the sake of truth!"

"You may be right." I sighed and looked through the tiny panes of glass once more. I wished I were already outside in the cold darkness. "I shall talk with Master Drake as soon as I can — perhaps, even tonight. No one will be more eager than he for Faith and me to quit Oxford . . . It probably would not be wise for me to come to the Two Ravens again . . . How can I send a message to you?"

"The boy who led you here will wait near Master Drake's house each noon. He is to be trusted, and he is clever."

"How old is he? Not more than ten, I think."

Jack smiled. "And therefore the less noticed."

I laughed and held out my hand to my friend, who rose as I approached him. "I shall be glad when I have grown up enough to be noticed," I said touching his shoulder. "We may not see each other again."

"But we shall! If not before, then when victory is ours."
Jack took one of the candlesticks from the mantelpiece to
light my way down the stairs.

"God be with you," I said.

Jack had opened the back door of the inn and was holding it ajar for me. The night was so still that the flame of
the candle burned undisturbed.

"May the cause of Parliament triumph," he whispered as
I stole out into the rubbish-filled yard.

By the corner of the house I waited until I heard the
door close and the bar of the lock slip into place. A terrible
feeling of loneliness came over me; I felt a despair far sharper
than I had ever experienced before. The Jack that I had
imagined and held conversations with in my mind when I
had been troubled was lost to me. No, worse than that,
he had never existed at all!

"The cause of Parliament," I whispered bitterly, as I
stepped from the narrow passageway into the street.

25
Tailor's Advice

When I returned from the Two Ravens, I found Master
Drake waiting for me. I told him of my adventures, but not
in the order in which they happened. First I related what I
had learned about Faith from Jack, then I recalled my conversation with the Provost Marshal, and finally, I told him
of my unlucky encounter with the Scottish Laird.

"The devil take that Scot! If he has fought for the Swedish King Gustav Adolphus, then he should be on our side,
not on that of King Charles." He frowned. "Methinks he
fought for gold."

I smiled. "If he did, then he never won, for he was poor
as any beggar when I met him at Ampthill."

"Are you sure he matched you with the boy he saw on
his journey?"

"At first I was not certain." I paused. To my surprise, the
tailor seemed eager for my answer to cast at least some doubt
that I had been recognized. I tried to conjure up the expression on the Scottish Laird's face, when he saluted me. "The
more I think of it, the more convinced I am ... He had a

knowing look, as if he had guessed a secret and was right pleased by it."

"Then I am afraid that your time in Oxford is over." Master Drake scratched his forehead. "I shall be sorry to see you leave, but if you are known then you will be more dangerous than useful."

There was a note of regret in the tailor's voice; and I responded to it by saying — and meaning it while I spoke — "I shall be sorry to leave, sir."

We were sitting in front of the fire in Master Drake's room. "I should not mind wearing your boots, Oliver." He bent down to stir up the blaze. "In a few days, you will be able to enter an inn, have a cup of cheer, and then speak your mind without fear of endangering your neck." He put the poker aside and looked at me. "No one knows until they have tried it, what a heavy burden it is not to be able to speak freely . . . They are not necessarily friends who serve the same cause. That is why I shall miss you, Oliver. It has been a rare treat for me to have someone in my house whom I trust and from whom I need not disguise my thoughts."

"It appears, sir, that you have disguised them only too well." This seemed to me the right moment to warn Master Drake of his daughter's fears.

He listened with wrinkled brow while I spoke, and when I finished he shook his head. "She thinks her father a thief or a dealer in stolen goods!" he exclaimed, astonished and indignant. "I who have never charged for an inch of cloth more than went into a coat."

"She guessed that more than sewing was going on under your roof, sir; and for that you cannot blame her. It is not usual for a master tailor to hire a boy to do errands and then spend hours locked in a room alone with him. The cook told her that I do little work for my keep, and the scullery maid says that I write the night away ... But there are other mysteries as well; people who come to your house at night, when — as she said — all honest men are abed."

For a while the tailor was silent, then suddenly he smiled wryly. "We should be thankful, Oliver, that they were so wide of the mark. My reputation for honesty will serve me well enough should the cook or the maid spread such a silly tale; especially since they are both known to be dull-witted. But my daughter is another matter ... For her own sake I cannot tell her too much; yet she must be told something."

"Aye," I agreed. "I think she suffers much."

"My wife ..." Master Drake paused, searching for words. "My wife would not harm the least of God's creatures. Tenderness came as natural to her as it is difficult for me ... I think it best I send my daughter to my sister ... I shall send my son as well."

I thought of the boy. Although I had seen him many times, I had never spoken to him. He may have been shy, but he seemed to regard all of the apprentices with a slight disdain, as if he could not bear the thought of being touched by any of us.

"The lass, is she full grown?"

I was startled by Master Drake's remark; and not understanding whom he meant, I shook my head. "Would she pass for a lad?" he asked a little irritably. "If the Marshal's men are looking for a girl, it might be wise to dress her up as a boy."

Finally I realized that the tailor was talking about Faith. "It is more than a year since I saw her last, but then she could have passed for a lad."

"The quicker we get the two of you to Aylesbury the better for all of us. You can leave her there. Colonel Mosley will find someone to take her in."

The idea of leaving Faith among strangers in Aylesbury had never occurred to me. "If I can, I shall take her with me to Huntingdon," I said.

"And what will General Cromwell say to that?" Master Drake grinned. "You are too young for marrying."

"Her father was . . . is my friend," I protested. "He let me stay at the Unicorn when I was not worth my keep."

"Colonel Mosley has a greater debt to Master Powers." The tailor touched my shoulder. "The girl will be a millstone round your neck. You have your way to make. You are only a boy, but with the General's help you may climb high."

I nodded and tried to smile. Master Drake was in earnest; there was no point in arguing with him. I could, after all, do as I pleased as soon as we were out of Oxford.

"I wish I were a youngster again . . . No tailor's needles for me, but I was born too late, by twenty years or more . . . My birthright was a pair of scissors; yours will be more than that. For when King and privilege are gone, then each man in this land shall fulfill the destiny which God meant for him!" Master Drake spoke heatedly. "Do not, Oliver, like so many fools, cripple yourself, so that you cannot enter the race. Leave the lass in Aylesbury, and hurry back to your General. And when you report to him, do not forget to mention my name."

I met the tailor's gaze. "That I shall, have no fear . . . Whatever I have done here of value, I could not have done without you . . . You have guided me, and much of the information that was in my letter to General Cromwell came from you."

"You are an honest lad . . . and clever, too." Master Drake spoke more calmly now. "And that is why I have warned you against doing a foolish act."

I smiled, and the tailor mistook my smile as approval of his views.

"Oliver, my lad, in ten years, I shall see you a Member of Parliament."

"If the Marshal's men don't snare me," I replied jestingly.

"Those cats are too fat to catch a sleek little mouse like you." The tailor grinned. "But if we could get both you and Master Powers's daughter out of town by tomorrow, so much the better. The Scottish Laird may have told about you, so speed is safety. In the morning, I shall talk to someone who might be able to help us. He is a farmer who has done me favors before. I think he knew your friend and will be more than willing to help his daughter."

A clock struck and we both sat silently counting the strokes of the bell. "Twelve, by God!" Master Drake exclaimed. "It is late. Tomorrow has become today; it is time for sleep, not talk."

I rose and started towards the door; but just as I was about to leave the room, the tailor called me back. "Oliver," he said, "it would be best if you stayed in the house from now on."

"I shall, sir," I answered and bade him good night. As I climbed the steps to my room, I suddenly remembered that I had forgotten, when I told Master Drake about Jack, to mention that my friend had wanted to meet him.

26
Faith

"My father wants you." Master Drake's daughter glanced round my room, and seemed surprised. It was tidy, and I was glad I had swept it that morning, although it had merely been a way of whiling away the time. When there had been nothing else to do, I had crept under the blankets of my bed with all my clothes on. It was bitterly cold.

"I shall come," I said politely and waited for her to go. But she remained standing in the doorway and finally, I sat up and started to draw on my boots.

"I know I have been a silly goose." She was blushing with embarrassment. "It is all the cook's fault. She told such stories ... And then ..."

"And then, you believed them," I replied hesitantly.

She looked at me defiantly. "If I had only had something else to believe, perhaps, I wouldn't have."

"I told your father that I thought you weren't to blame." I stamped the heel of my boot on the floor, pulled at the sides, and my foot slipped into place.

"How could I have guessed that he was assisting the King,

by keeping an eye on all those who have come to Oxford for the parliament?"

I couldn't hide my surprise; but she misunderstood the astonishment plainly visible on my face. "Oh, I know that I am not to tell anyone. And I won't either," she declared.

"No, that is best kept a secret," I muttered, wondering whether it had been wise of the tailor to tell such lies to his daughter.

"You can trust me," she said, and, for the first time, Master Drake's daughter gave me a friendly smile.

When I entered his room, I found her father in excellent humor. He was beaming, as if the sun had been shining on all his ventures. "We are in luck!" he exclaimed, as soon as I had closed the door behind me. "And luck is a cross-eyed goddess who will often smile at your enemies when you need her most."

"You have found someone who will take us past sentries?" I asked.

"Aye," he replied. "I met the very farmer that I told you about, in the very first place that I looked for him. He is a most trustworthy person; and what is more important, no one suspects him of being more than he appears — an honest farmer who can supply fat geese and lean beef."

My hands were numb with cold and I took a few steps closer to the fireplace. "Well, I am ready to leave."

"If your friend can bring the girl here at two, you shall both be out of Oxford before nightfall."

"A beggar boy is supposed to be here at midday. But the clocks have not struck twelve yet."

The tailor was standing before the window. "Does that boy have ears that stick out from his head, as if they had been pulled once too often?" Master Drake grinned. "For if that is so, I think he has come early."

I rushed to the window. "Yes, that is he," I said, looking down at the urchin, and thinking, "His feet are still bare; he must be very cold."

"You will talk to him alone. I do not want him to know more than he might have already guessed." The tailor was gazing thoughtfully at the boy. "Tell him to bring Faith here a little before the clock strikes two, dressed as a boy, if that is possible. They are to wait for you a little further down the street. They are not to come to this house or to see me at all."

"I shall explain," I said and started towards the door.

"Hurry, I'll watch you from here. He shouldn't stand there too long."

"I must go to my room first," I apologized, "but I shall be quick about it."

"Why?" Master Drake asked.

"I . . . I need a shilling," I mumbled with embarrassment.

The tailor threw me a sixpence and laughed. "That will do for him. If you give him more, you might make a cavalier out of him."

As soon as he saw me, the boy looked at me expectantly.

I recognized the expression on his face, as I crossed the street. I had seen it before on younger boys, when older ones lowered themselves enough to include them in their plans.

I smiled at the urchin and he grinned back. Had he been a puppy and had a tail, it would have been wagging. When I gave him my instructions, his head nodded at every word to show his eagerness to obey.

"You must be here shortly before the clock strikes two," I repeated my last command and dropped the sixpence into his hand. He closed it into a fist immediately, as if he feared he might lose the coin; then he ran down the street in the direction that I had taken when I had walked to the Two Ravens.

I had little appetite for the midday meal, which we all ate together. I heard the laughter of the apprentices but not what caused it. I was thinking of Faith, wondering what she would be like. Had she grown? Would she still be the child who had once asked me to marry her? I was beginning to understand that the task I had taken on might not be an easy one.

Long before the appointed time, I was at the window, watching the street, much to the amusement of Master Drake.

"Faith," the tailor drawled. "I have never liked these names which supply you with a character at birth. I think a lass who has been given such a name should be a proper infidel and prove herself untrue to all."

"As I remember her," I replied smilingly, "she is a very good little girl."

"That was a year ago or more," Master Drake grinned. "You were probably a good little boy then, too."

"What if she refuses to leave Oxford because her father is still a prisoner in the Castle?" I asked anxiously. "I am not sure that I would leave, if Master Powers were my father."

The pleasant expression on Master Drake's face changed to one of deep annoyance. "Nonsense! She is more of a danger to her father than anything else! And to other good folks as well. A daughter must obey, even if she has had a score of birthdays ... So must a son."

Obviously the tailor's daughter had not wanted to be sent to her aunt. But then it must have been difficult for Master Drake to explain the reason why her departure was necessary, if he were a spy for King Charles.

"Still, it must be hard for Faith," I said.

There was a group of soldiers passing in the street; and for a moment, I was filled with terror; but they walked on without even glancing at Master Drake's house, and inwardly I smiled at my own nervousness. "She has no one but her father," I remarked when the street was empty again.

"Now she has you!" the tailor bantered. His irritation was forgotten. "If she cries you must kiss her tears away like a true gallant."

I sighed, for that was exactly what I feared: that Faith would cry. And how would I stop her tears? Not by kissing them away like a gallant, for that I had neither the age nor the skill.

"You cannot miss the farmer. He is the biggest man in Oxfordshire and as strong as an ox. His cart will be at the gate to All Souls." This was the third time that Master Drake had repeated his instructions.

"I will find him." I peered through the little glass pane; it felt cold against my forehead.

There was the boy! He had returned alone. Something had gone wrong!

"Master Drake!" I called and the tailor came quickly to my side. "It is the beggar . . ." But as I said the words, I realized that I was wrong, it was someone else wearing the rags that the urchin had worn.

"She will pass as a lad, but she is younger than I expected." The tailor was smiling, and suddenly I felt a violent dislike for Master Drake.

Faith had pressed herself against the wall of a house a few steps down the street on the opposite side. Even from where I was standing, I could sense her fear and despair. "I must go!" I declared and made my way to the door and lifted the latch, without even saying good-bye to Master Drake.

"Wait, Oliver," the tailor stopped me. "I want you to take this." He held out a golden sovereign.

"I have no need of it," I said curtly. My anger had not completely disappeared.

"But it is yours." Master Drake winked. "You have stolen it."

"Stolen it!" I exclaimed in great confusion.

"Oh yes," he said as he pressed the coin into my hand. "That is what I am going to tell the apprentices and the cook. I shall blacken your character in this house, for safety's sake."

"You mean in case I get caught, and nightfall finds me inside Oxford Castle instead of on the road to Aylesbury?"

"Oh no!" the tailor protested unhappily. "It is merely to stop everyone wondering why you went away."

"If I have stolen it," I said a little shamefacedly, "then I might as well have it." As I slipped the coin into my purse, I noticed that Master Drake was smiling again; and I realized that he enjoyed his devious lying. "One day," I thought, "it may bring him into trouble."

"The lass will need some clothes when you get to Aylesbury," he said. "No one will take her in; the way she looks you could not even marry her to a broom." The tailor's hand rested on my shoulder. He pressed it gently, and then gave me a little shove out of the room.

"Oliver?" Faith pronounced my name as if she were not really sure that I was the boy she had known.

"Come," I said, and took her hand. "There is a farmer

with a cart waiting for us near the gate to All Souls; he has promised to take us out of Oxford."

Obediently, the girl walked beside me. I looked down at her; she was almost a head shorter than I was. I had expected her face to be tear-stained, but it was not. "Will you take me with you?" she asked. "Always?"

"Yes," I muttered guiltily, for I felt far from certain that I would be able to protect her. One word from Colonel Mosley in Aylesbury, and she would be taken from me.

"That is good," the little girl said very seriously, "for I want to stay with you."

27
A Fugitive

The cart was only a few yards from the gate to All Souls. The driver was busily adjusting the harness of his mare. Suddenly he straightened himself and looked around. He was truly a giant of a man.

"There he is," I whispered to Faith. "For surely there are not two men of his size in all of England."

"I know him — he came often to my father's inn." A thin smile passed over the girl's face, like a single line of sunshine that sometimes appears in an overcast sky and is swiftly gone.

"Come, be quick, you have kept me waiting," the farmer said sharply, when he saw us; but the expression on his face belied his tone of voice. "The days are still short, and we must hurry if we are to be home by nightfall."

"I am sorry," I said, trying to make my voice match my words, though it was almost impossible for me not to smile, for the man was to my liking.

"You can ride," he said roughly to Faith. "But your brother has stout boots and can walk with me." The giant

picked Faith up and lifted her over the side of the cart; then
he grabbed the reins and clicked his tongue.

The mare shook her head, as if to answer him, and we
started on our way. The metal wheels rattled loudly against
the cobblestones of the street.

"My farm is one mile east of Thame; my family has held
it since the time of King Henry the Eighth," he said proudly.
"And they call me Master Goodwyn."

"My name is Oliver Cutter," I said breathlessly; I had
difficulty keeping up with him. "And I own no more land
but what dirt by chance might be beneath my nails."

"Then there will be little enough to plow in springtime."
Master Goodwyn chuckled over his own wit.

Faith was looking at me, and I smiled back. "If I did not
know better, even I would take her for a boy," I thought
with relief.

"The lass owns even less," I said to the farmer. "There
are those who would not let her keep her life."

"I know her father; he is an honest man." Master Goodwyn stared grimly in front of him. "I am only too pleased
to do him a service . . . When we come to the gate, let me
speak for all three of us. I am well known to the sentries."

But I was not to get out of Oxford that day. As I turned
my gaze from Master Goodwyn, I saw in the distance, coming rapidly towards us, the Scottish Laird and three of the
Marshal's men!

Oh, how much can pass through your mind at such a

moment! I remember thinking, "Birds of a feather flock together," and warning Faith, whose head was sticking up above the sides of the cart, to duck.

Just as the Laird broke into a run, shouting, "Stop thief! Stop that boy!" I managed to lean down and whisper loud enough for Faith to hear me, "I will come for you. Do not despair!" Then I started running faster than I ever had run before. I was running for my life!

As I darted behind him, I heard Master Goodwyn mumble, "God bless and protect you, boy."

I ran down the first alley I came to; but I was so scared that it might end in a wall too high for me to climb that when I spied an open door to a garden I dived through it and closed it behind me.

The garden was small, and at one point the wall which surrounded it was so low that I could vault it. As I scrambled down the other side, I found myself in a slightly larger garden. There was no one about; all was silence. The windows of the college looked like so many blind eyes. The other walls were too high for me to scale without a ladder, but there was an arched opening, closed by an iron gate. Through its bars I could see a lane, which surely must lead somewhere. It was locked, but between the spikes of the door and the gateway was just space enough for me to squeeze through.

The lane led out into Broad Street near Balliol College. It was filled with people, some going about their business but others who had no errands. They were there to be en-

tertained by whatever might happen. It was these loafers —
most of them soldiers — of whom I was frightened. They
were ready for any amusement which would make their day
less tedious. A cry of "Stop thief!" and they would all glee-
fully join in the chase.

I felt as if every eye were scrutinizing my face. Where
was I to go? I could not return to Master Drake's; the tailor
might have already accused me of thievery to his apprentices. But even if he hadn't, it would not be fair of me to
endanger him. As for Jack and the Two Ravens, would I
be welcome there? Oh, my friend would try to hide me,
that I did not doubt; but had I any right to hazard his safety?

Near Bishop King's palace were some humbler buildings,
where artisans lived. I made my way towards them, hoping
there to find someplace to hide until dark. I entered a small
tavern. It was deserted, and the girl who offered to serve
me did not seem to take much interest in me. In a corner,
not far from the door, I sat down on a bench.

Only when I bit into the bread, did I realize how hungry
I was. The cheese was dry and hard as a rock, but the ale
helped me to swallow it.

My mind was as empty as a summer sky, but not as
pleasant. How would I get out of Oxford? I did not even
know the password; that was changed every day — at least
so I had been told. Nor could I climb the walls of the town;
besides they were patrolled.

I took out my purse. Among the silver, gold glistened.
There were two sovereigns and almost a pound in silver.

Could I bribe someone to let me pass? I selected a shilling with which to pay for my food, and tied my purse strings. Bribery was not an easy course. Anyone who was willing to take my money might be as willing to betray me in the hope of getting an even larger sum.

With a loud clanging of their metal-shod boots, a group of soldiers entered, among them some of the Provost Marshal's men! I wanted to get up and run; but that would have been the most foolish thing I could have done. I crouched in my corner, hoping I looked no different from any apprentice trying to avoid his master, or farmer's lad waiting for his father.

The Marshal's men shouted their orders, as if the world were deaf. They were as arrogant as butcher's dogs. When they weren't cursing, they were grumbling.

"The end of a rope would be the proper payment for such beasts," I thought. Looking at them I envisioned Master Powers, with his bright, intelligent eyes. "Crook-back," they called him. It was unbearable to think of his being tortured, with only such pitiless men as these to hope for mercy from. "Could the Scottish Laird be such a brute?" No, I could not imagine him glorying in that kind of baseness. Although he was the cause of my plight, I did not hate him. He had come to Oxford on a stolen horse, with only the few shillings he had received for the pewter he had stolen from the inn at Ampthill. He was old, and his long service with the Swedish King Gustav Adolphus, who was an enemy of King Charles, would not recommend him to the cavaliers. When he had recognized me in the street, he had remembered what a different figure I had cut at the inn. And he probably thought, "Here is a thread of a tangled web, let me catch hold of it; and if it can be unraveled, who knows but that I might have done a service worthy of a royal reward." True or not, this explanation satisfied me.

I ordered more ale, not because I wanted it but because I thought it best to stay in the corner, unnoticed, until the soldiers had left.

The windows darkened. The inn-keeper put two tallow candles on the beam above the fireplace. The tavern was crowded now; the Marshal's men were still there, but I could easily slip out unseen by them. As soon as I stood up, my place on the bench was immediately taken.

There was still a little light in the sky, but soon the night would be as black as the devil's hide.

28
A Cold Night's Lodging

There were still people in the street but fewer than before; and those who braved the cold evening air were intent on some business. They walked briskly and were not inclined to notice their fellow wanderers. Their pinched noses and frozen ears told them to hurry to their destinations.

I imitated them and walked swiftly, though I had no goal nor any fire to look forward to. I envied all of them, even the apprentices scurrying home to a master from whom they might receive a beating, for they, at least, would have a warm corner to sleep in that night. The sky was clear; and all the stars were shining brightly, for the moon had not risen yet. I passed several soldiers. There were guards on the streets. Now they did not even look at me; but later, would they not wonder who I was and ask me where I lived? I tried to think of some plausible errand that I could have been sent on in the middle of the night. But even if I had no reason to fear anyone's curiosity, I could not roam the streets until daybreak; I would be frozen to death by then. No, I decided that I must find some shelter.

How difficult it is to search, and at the same time not appear to be doing so. There was enough thievery in Oxford for people to be very wary of anyone who seemed to inspect their property too closely. Another danger was dogs; most can be cajoled with a calm word, but there are those so ferocious that even their masters are hardly safe from their jaws.

In the darkness all buildings are merely black shadows; but I kept not only my eyes open but my nose as well. A good dunghill revealed that there was a stable nearby; and no companions are better than cows or horses, especially on a cold night, if you have no fire or bedclothes.

The streets were almost deserted, when I finally found what I had been looking for. It was a shed in back of a small house. A cart in the yard between the house and the stable assured me that I would find a horse within. No light shone from any of the windows. Everyone had gone to bed, but were they all asleep?

I stood long, pressed against the wall of the house, listening. All was silent. The moon had risen and the yard was bathed in moonlight. In front of the shed was a pile of manure. My heart was beating so loudly that I felt sure half the world could hear it.

Slowly, I crept along the wall to the entrance of the stable. It was closed with a simple iron latch. I opened the door noiselessly, prepared to flee if I heard a growl.

The warmth soothed my fears; I stepped inside and closed

the door behind me. I could hear the breathing of the horses in their stalls. One shook its head and a chain rustled. Now to find where the hay was kept; once snuggled inside it, I could sleep until sunrise.

Something put me on my guard; perhaps it was only fear. It was hard to believe that I had been so lucky. There was something wrong! Keeping my hand outstretched in front of me, I took a few steps forward. Suddenly the warmth of the stable was gone, and I trembled with terror. My finger-tips had touched the face of a man!

"Stand still or I'll cut your throat," a low voice grunted.

I was too panic stricken to do anything but obey. Still without knowing it, I did take one small step backwards.

"I told you to stand still!" A hand grasped my shoulder and pulled me forward. "I have killed so many men that it is long since I lost count of the number." The man had been drinking; I could smell it on his breath. "Who are you?" he asked in a hoarse tone.

"Oliver . . ." I stammered. "Oliver Cutter . . . I am . . . I am only a boy seeking shelter for the night."

A snarl that would have seemed more fitting had it come from an animal's throat greeted my words.

"I had no place to sleep and I feared I would freeze to death," I explained to the unknown man in the darkness.

"Come!" The strong hand which held my shoulder dragged me to the back of the stable, where a ladder led to the loft. Pushing me against it, he ordered, "Climb!"

The sweet smell of hay filled my nostrils. How happy I would have been had I climbed this ladder undiscovered. Now, terrified, I stepped out onto the floor of the loft.

"Sit down!" he commanded as roughly as before.

A spark flew and the man blew on the tinder; then carefully, he lighted a tiny stump of a candle. Now at least I would see my murderer.

The face the light made it possible for me to see was not as horrible as I had imagined it would be. The wrinkles around the eyes told that sometimes it had smiled. I could not believe that it was my murderer I was looking at.

This may have shown in my expression, for my captor frowned; but then as he held the candle closer to me, he started to laugh. "Have you run away from your master to escape a thrashing?" he asked.

"Aye," I lied hastily enough. "I work for a farmer named Master Goodwyn, and I ran away from him this afternoon, when we brought some sheep to town. But then it got dark and I had nowhere to go."

The man chuckled. "It is easy to run away in your dreams. The nights are never cold and roast partridges hang from the trees. But you'd be glad to be with your master now, wouldn't you?"

"Yes," I agreed fervently.

"Well, you can go home in the morning and bring him a switch for a present. Is he a hard master, does he ask for much work and give you little food?"

"No," I replied, "I have been foolish." I was wondering

what to say that would please the man most. "I thought I could become a soldier."

"A soldier!" He roared with laughter. "That would be the life! And did you think that the King would make you a general?"

"No." I tried to look as humble as I could. "But now I am afraid that they won't let me through the gates."

"They usually don't bother with the likes of you. Just tell them you are going home to your master." The man's face grew thoughtful. "You have not been stealing, have you?"

"No!" I exclaimed indignantly. "I am not a thief!"

"I did not say you were, so keep your temper, I don't want it. But there is enough around who would cut a throat for a shilling."

"That is true," I agreed, and my fear returned: Could he be one of them?

"I keep the horses and sleep here at night, to make the place safe from the likes of you." He scowled as if he were debating whether he ought to tell his master that I was there.

"All I want is to sleep the night," I begged. "I will leave at daybreak."

The man nodded. "There will be no harm in that I suppose." Then he smiled. "I ran away twice when I was a boy to escape a beating but only caught a worse one."

"Oh, that I too will get!" I agreed, since the thought of my being flogged obviously pleased the old fellow. "My master has a temper like a bear."

"They call me Rob," he said, and put his hand down

heavily on my shoulder. "Bury yourself in the hay, and you will be warm enough."

"Thank you," I said. "And God bless you."

"I shall wake you in the morning. I would not want my master to see you." Rob watched me burrow myself into the pile of hay nearest the ladder; then he blew out the candle and climbed down.

I could hear him below me. "He sleeps near the horses," I thought, "but then it is warmer there."

"Good night," he called. "Tomorrow night when your back is sore, you will be sleeping on your stomach."

"Good night," I shouted back, while I wondered why so many old men took so much pleasure in telling youngsters about the beatings they would get.

A thistle in the hay pricked my neck. I groped for it in the darkness. "No one has ever slept in a sweeter smelling bed," I thought. "But how am I to escape from Oxford?"

The sentries certainly would not let me through the gates. Whatever the Scottish Laird had told the Provost Marshal's men ensured that. "May he roast in hell, and may the devil's grandmother turn the spit," I mumbled, and my curse made me grin.

"At least Faith is safe," I thought. I was the one that the Scottish Laird and the louts who were with him had run after. As for the guards, Master Goodwyn was a match for them.

I yawned. Sleep was coming. Tomorrow would have to take care of itself.

29

The King's Duty

"Get up!" Rob was shaking me. For a moment, I did not know where I was; then everything that had happened yesterday came tumbling back through my mind. I groaned, which made Rob laugh.

"Get you up! The maid has lit the fire in the house and soon the master will be up and about." The man appeared to be no more than a shadow, but there was a dim grayness in the loft. It must be after dawn.

Wearily, I climbed down the ladder. Through the open half-door, I could see the overcast winter sky. I turned to thank Rob. This was the first time that I actually saw clearly any part of him but his face. In the flame of the tallow candle, last night, he had seemed a very large man. Now I realized that he was small. He limped; one of his legs was much shorter than the other. But his hands were large and strong, as I knew so well from the time he had grabbed me in the darkness.

Smilingly, he wished me good luck, and in parting made

one more reference to the beating I would get from my master.

Before I stepped out into the street, I brushed the hay from my clothes. I was thinking of Rob; and why it so often was a simple or a deformed man who took care of horses: someone marked from birth, in a manner which set him apart from others. I smiled, recalling his boast that he had killed so many men that he had lost count of the number. I doubted that he had ever killed anything beyond a horsefly that had stung his favorite animal. "Oh, that was it! Now I know," I thought. "The horse is the most beautiful of all beasts, and if you treat it kindly, it will always return your affection." No one loved the Robs of this world, but they needed love, as everyone else does; and therefore, they took care of horses. I remembered how many times I had gone to the stable to talk to my mare when something had happened that was not to my liking.

The day was warmer; there was a change in the air. I knew of a place where bread was sold. "I might as well eat before I am hanged," I decided.

Still chewing the warm bread, I walked towards the eastern gate of the city. This was the busiest entrance to Oxford and the most carefully watched; for the country to the east was not held by the Royalists, and it was from that direction that a Parliamentary attack was most feared.

Already there was traffic on the road. I took a stand far enough away from the portal not to be noticed by the soldiers. I was most eager to see what happened to those who wished to depart. A cart approached the sentries. A boy and a man were walking beside it. The child was younger than I. The wagon was ransacked; and, from the gatehouse, someone came out to look at the boy. I turned away and started walking slowly in the opposite direction.

"Oh, they are looking for me," I thought. "There can be no doubt about it." I heard the rattling of the wheels; the cart had been allowed to pass.

A young man galloping as fast as he could rode past me. I stepped aside, and, without thinking, turned once more to stare at the sentries. The one who had looked at the boy was no longer outside.

As the rider approached the gate, he checked his horse to a trot and called out clearly, "On the service of the King." Then he leaned over and said something else, which I could not hear.

"The password of the day," I thought, and cursed that I did not have sharper ears.

Everyone got out of his way. The young man spurred his horse and galloped through the gate.

Where was I to go? I decided that I should make my way to the southern gate, which, being very narrow and having much less traffic, was not so heavily guarded.

There, by chance, I did learn the password! Two splendidly dressed cavaliers, who seemed to be leaving for a day's hunting, did loudly and arrogantly cry out to the soldiers:

"The King's duty!" which made the sentries bow low and remove their caps.

I wandered the streets; my thoughts seemed to travel in circles like a caged beast.

It was midmorning when I was hailed near Christ Church by a cry of, "Boy, come here!"

I looked around, prepared to flee; but it was the Irish Lord who had given me a shilling two days before. He was just dismounting from the loveliest horse I had ever seen. I ran up to him and made a slight bow.

He grinned and, handing me the reins, he said, "If you are not afraid of a horse, boy, then hold him for me till I come back."

"I am not, sir." Very gently I touched the animal's neck. As smooth as velvet was its skin.

"But do not try to ride him. He will break your neck; only an Irishman can master him!" With a proud smile, the young man gazed affectionately at his horse.

"I shan't, sir," I replied. Following his glance, I realized that the horse was a stallion.

"I shall return soon, and you shall have another shilling," the Lord said cheerfully as he walked towards Christ Church.

"You are a handsome boy," I whispered to my charge, as I scratched his head. The horse sniffed me, as if to find out what kind of animal I was. His breath was warm and sweet; and I could not help laughing as we rubbed noses like two strange horses meeting in a field.

The stallion seemed satisfied that I meant him no harm,

for he nudged me several times. He was dappled, gray and white, with a muzzle as pink as a young girl's lips.

I began to feel hopeful. Could I not somehow persuade the Irish Lord to help me? I was trying to make up a proper tale to tell him, when I saw two of Master Drake's apprentices in the distance. I was about to wave, when one of them called: "Stop the thief!"

I suppose I could have let go of the Irishman's horse and run, but that never occurred to me. I jumped on the stallion, dug my heels into his side, and galloped down the street.

As fast as the wind, making everyone I met leap for his life, through the unguarded gate of the old walls I went; then out into the open field, across the bridge that spanned the river. Ahead was the eastern gate and beyond that the road to Aylesbury and to safety.

"On the King's service!" I screamed loudly as I approached.

Two soldiers tried to bar my way. "The King's duty!" I called. "Make way! Make way!"

The password was correct and this confused the sentries. They stepped aside and I caught a glimpse of their astonished faces, as I thundered past.

"I'm free! I'm free!" I shouted at the wind as it whistled by.

30

A Ride to Freedom

The mare that I rode in Huntingdon was considered a fine
animal: fast and sure-footed. But she was an old broken-
winded beast compared to the Irishman's stallion. The stirrups of the saddle were too long for my legs, but there was
no time to adjust them now, when I expected at any moment
to be given chase by a pack of Royal soldiers. Besides, so
long as I was galloping it did not matter, for the stallion
had a seat that would have suited an old woman. With
easy movements he tore over the road, and it felt almost as
though we were flying. I leaned forward and told the beast
how much I loved him. Horses like softly spoken words,
for in their strong bodies are gentle souls. "You are a brave
boy ... You are a brave boy," I whispered and the stallion
snorted as if he understood me.

Not before the roads to Aylesbury and High Wycombe
part company did I stop my wild ride. By this time the
stallion was sweating and his bit was covered with foam.
As I clapped his neck, he looked at me as if to ask what it
was all about. I told the horse that he would have to save

me, for my enemies were after me, which made the animal turn his head and look back, as though he wanted to catch a glimpse of our pursuers. In truth, I believed that given the choice at the crossroads, the cavaliers would think that I had taken the road to High Wycombe because this led to London. Though they still might send a few troopers towards Aylesbury as well, I had the lead, and it would be difficult for them to catch up with me. Now I took the time to shorten the stirrups.

The saddle and bridle were worthy of the horse. "All who see me must wonder how a boy so poorly dressed came to be so splendidly mounted," I thought. At first I had planned to abandon the stallion in some field, and make most of my way on foot; for I had feared that riding such a horse would make me too conspicuous. But now, I would as soon have parted with my life.

As I trotted towards Thame, I grew less and less frightened of meeting cavaliers; yet when I saw two horsemen approach me, I was prepared for the worst. As they came nearer I realized that they were troopers of the Parliamentary army. But my relief was shortlived, for these were Lord Essex's men, and his soldiers were ready and rough and had no discipline.

They hailed me and their horses blocked the road. "Well, my lad," one of them began gruffly, "where would you be going?" He was by far the older of the two; the other was so young as to be not many years a man.

"To Aylesbury," I replied, holding the stallion back, yet ready to leap between them.

"A pretty war-horse for a nursling like you to ride." The man grinned. "Methinks that beast best fits a man."

"Aye, that be so," I agreed. "I am bringing it to my master, General Cromwell." I hoped the name of the General would make them fearful of waylaying me, but it only made them laugh.

"My lad, a general can have his pick of horses, whereas a poor trooper like meself must ride what I can get." Suddenly he stopped smiling and shouted, "Get off that horse, boy!"

I tried to turn the stallion, but the horses of the soldiers wedged me in. The older man bent forward to take my reins, when without warning he screamed as if all the fiends of hell had grabbed him.

It was not as bad as that, though the bite my stallion had taken of his thigh must have felt as piercing as a devil's fork. His scream terrified his horse, and she shied away, leaving the road open for me to pass.

Loudly whinnying, the stallion rose on his hind legs, pawing the air with his two front hoofs, as if he meant to mount the sky. I almost fell off.

"Away!" I shouted, letting loose the reins. And away we went, so fast that I believed that if they had shot at me, we would have outridden their bullets.

A few miles before Thame, I asked a man who was driving a cow in the direction of the town if he knew where Master Goodwyn's farm was.

He looked at me and then at my horse. "That's a powerful beast," he said instead of answering my question.

"Aye," I agreed. "He is that."

The man scratched his ear and then took a step forward, because his cow had not stopped and was walking on ahead. "About a half mile to the north," he finally replied. "There's a clump of willow trees, where you turn for his lane."

I thanked him and smiled. It was lucky his cow had not started grazing in the ditch, for he seemed bent on holding a conversation.

I saw the willows from afar. As I trotted along the path I noted that on either side were fine fields. Master Goodwyn was not a poor man.

The house was large and the farm buildings well kept. There was an air of order; and as I dismounted a stable-boy came towards me. Then he stood still, gaping at my mount, as though I had been riding a lion.

"Is your master at home?" I asked; but before he had time to answer, a woman came out of the door of the dwelling. "This is Master Goodwyn's goodwife," I thought and made a bow. "My name is Oliver Cutter and I have an errand with your husband."

The woman looked at me suspiciously, and returned to the house. A moment later Master Goodwyn appeared, but Faith darted out before him. I was relieved to see that she was no longer wearing the rags in which she had escaped from Oxford, but was dressed like a proper farmer's lass.

She called my name over and over again. I put my arm around her; the poor girl was crying.

"And where did you get a great beast like that from?" Master Goodwyn was circling my mount, eyeing it as a miser would a heap of gold.

"I borrowed it from an Irish Lord," I said with a grin.

"Get ye gone!" Mistress Goodwyn screamed at me. "And take the lass with ye!"

The huge man frowned angrily, but he said nothing.

"I have three lads of me own, besides a lass. They be your own blood and all the very spit of you," she shouted.

"Every sow thinks its brood the best," Master Goodwyn said sourly.

"Aye," returned his wife, enraged, "and who will help them if you be hanged and the farm burned down?"

I smiled reassuringly to Faith. "We are going, Mistress."

"I shall show you the way that will take you around Thame," Master Goodwyn offered.

"God be with you," his wife mumbled. Now, suddenly, she seemed ashamed, as if, having won her point, she wished she had not had to argue at all. She muttered something more which I did not hear and disappeared into the house.

"I should not have minded keeping you for a day or two," Master Goodwyn remarked with embarrassment. "I have a mare down in the meadow who has a hankering above her station, and I would have bred them." He made one final circle round the stallion, and shook his head with admiration.

When I had mounted, he seated Faith behind me. I told

her to put her hands around my waist and hold on; then, with Master Goodwyn leading the way, we took the path across the fields. The stallion, who had shown himself to have a temper as ferocious as his size, walked gently, as if he knew that now he was also carrying a young girl.

"There yonder by the copse of fir trees," Master Goodwyn pointed to a tiny woods in the distance, "there you will meet the road to Aylesbury."

"Thank you," I said. "And God be with you."

"And God be with you, too, my boy." The farmer looked down at the ground and then up at me again. "I would have kept the lass, but she will be safer elsewhere. Here we as often see cavaliers as we do soldiers of Parliament." Then he added in a rush, "My wife's heart is as sound as the bell in the church at Thame. It is because of her love for the little ones."

I nodded to show that I understood and he need say no more, then Faith thanked him for the clothes he had given her.

"I could not have let ye travel, half-naked as you were," he protested with a laugh.

Once more we said good-bye; and when we had ridden a bit, I turned around and waved. Master Goodwyn was still standing where we had left him.

"When we came, she would not let me in," Faith whispered.

"You cannot blame her," I replied. "If either of us had been caught in their house, they would have fared ill."

"But the night was so dark and cold." There was a tremor in the girl's voice, and I turned around to get a glimpse of her face.

"But now you are here with me," I said and smiled. Faith pressed herself against me. "The shadows are getting longer," I thought. "We will be lucky to make Aylesbury by nightfall."

31
Aylesbury

It was dark when we entered Aylesbury, and a light flurry of snow was falling. We were not even questioned by the sentries, which suited me well, though it hardly recommended the commandant as a soldier. I made my way to Tom the carter's house, hopeful that he would shelter both the horse and ourselves. Child that I still was, I wanted to change into my finery which I had left with him.

Tom was at home and much surprised to see me. "I heard the Provost Marshal skinned you and made a pair of boots from your hide," he chided, though in truth his broad smile showed that he was glad that I was back in Aylesbury. He was not a man to speak of his sentiments; and the nearest he came to it was when he welcomed Faith with the words: "Your father sold me many a good pot of ale . . . England can ill-afford to lose such an honest inn-keeper, they being as scarce, in my opinion, as angels are in hell!"

Tom did not seem to notice that the only reply to his witticism was Faith's silent stare; nor did she cross the threshold of his house, until the carter's wife, who was a square little body with a laughing head, stepped out and put her arm around the girl's shoulders to draw her in.

Although Tom was not easy to impress, he was for once speechless when I took him outside to show him my mount. He whistled slowly as he viewed the stallion. The great horse stood very still; his bridle was tied to a fence.

"Aye, you are not for me," he finally said. "Too grand by far for Tom . . . Did you steal the King's horse, Oliver?"

"No, he belongs to an Irish Lord."

"Well, if he was fairly stolen, right under his nose, then he's yours now." The carter grinned. "But you might have trouble keeping him, for I would say that even our Colonel's mouth will water when he sees him."

"I am bringing him back for General Cromwell," I said as if this had always been my plan, although, in truth, I should have liked to keep him. "Can you house him in your stable tonight?"

"If your stallion does not mind such humble company as my little beast, he is welcome." Tom scratched his thigh. "It be wise of you to say that you are bringing him to your General. He is a great man that no one likes to cross."

We gave the horse some hay and a handful of oats. As I took off the saddle and bridle, the carter laughed and said, "Colonel Mosley does not have as fine a one as that. Such a saddle no one in Aylesbury can make."

I decided to wait until morning to see the Colonel. I hoped that my old gelding was still alive and that he would give it to me for Faith to ride.

When we sat down to our supper, Faith insisted upon sitting next to me. She hardly spoke, even to me; and only when I smiled at her did she smile timidly back. I would have to stand by her. This was my fate. Although it frightened me, it also made me strangely happy. Before she died, my mother had begged me to stay with my father and help him. That was a promise which I had not been able to keep. Somewhere, in some tavern, at that very moment, my father was probably shipwrecked in an ocean of ale. To save my father from himself was a task beyond my strength. But by not deserting Faith and taking care that no harm came to her, I felt in some mysterious way that I was keeping my word to my mother.

"I have heard all about you!" Colonel Mosley grinned. "Stealing horses and saving maidens in distress."

I shrugged my shoulders and smiled. To my surprise, the Colonel had called me in before a young lieutenant who had been waiting for an audience with him as well.

"And what do you think General Cromwell will think of these wild deeds of yours?"

"I am bringing him the horse as a gift," I said.

"By the devil!" the Colonel cursed. "I thought you would sell the stallion to me. I have heard that it is a rare, fine animal." Then he spoke good-naturedly again, "By God, boy, I would have you join my troops, so you could bring me a gift like that. Whom did it belong to?"

I had been trying to remember the title of the Irish noble-

man, but I couldn't recall it. "I think ... I think ..." I
finally stammered, convinced that what I was about to say
was wrong. "They called him Lord Inch of the Queen."

The Colonel roared with laughter and repeated the title
several times, as my face grew red with shame and I wished
that I had been born without the gift of speech.

"An inch of the Queen, that treacherous Irishman probably
is; and he would kiss both hers and the King's toe. But for
all that he is a brave soldier. I have heard of him. His title
is Lord Inchiquin; and whether we hang him under that name
or O'Brien, which he is also called, is all the same to
me."

"I do not know whether he would kiss a royal toe, but I
do know that he has no chance of doing it," I said and described to the Colonel my meeting with the Irish Lord.

When I had finished, he remarked, "It seems to be that
Charles is the greatest fool that ever wore a crown. He flings
aside able men and dotes upon dolts. Though Lord Inchiquin
is my enemy, I cannot help but feel sorry for him. To lose
royal favor and your horse seems hard." The Colonel grinned
again. "By God, Oliver, you were wise. It is seldom worth it
to cut an Irishman's purse, but to steal his horse is another
matter, for an Irish chieftain is more particular when he picks
his horse than when he chooses his wife."

"I have never seen a finer horse than that stallion," I said
with pride.

"Then since you will not sell it to me, I shall not look at

him. Envy — I am told most Sundays from the pulpit — is one of the most serious sins."

"The gelding which I brought from Huntingdon, is that still here?" I asked hesitantly.

"He pined away, as soon as you left," the Colonel drawled, with mock sadness. "It was a great pity, for we are so short of horses. But if you should be in need of another, then go back to Oxford and steal Prince Rupert's. He, I believe, rides a mare, and then you will have one of each kind, like Noah."

It seemed that Colonel Mosley liked to sharpen his wits on his subordinates, and they always make convenient but poor grindstones. "I wanted the gelding for the girl; I know he was of little use, but he might have been able to carry her," I explained.

"Ah, the girl!" Colonel Mosley rubbed his hands together. "Are you going to give her to the General as well? That may not be to his wife's liking."

"No, I shall keep her, sir," I said sternly. "She is still a child."

"The budding rose is more beautiful than the flower in bloom." The Colonel winked.

My temper was mounting, and I said as politely as I could that Faith could ride pillion behind me, and that we would be leaving the following morning.

"I am sending some wagons for supplies to Cambridge. They will be an escort as well; you will be safer with them. Who knows, Lord Inchiquin may be looking for his horse."

"Thank you," I said and bowed. At least for the first part of the journey, I preferred traveling in company.

"It is no inconvenience. The wagons are empty. In my stable, you will find saddle blankets, and you may wrap the girl in one of them. The weather is still cold." The Colonel looked at me thoughtfully. "*Cromwell's boy* — that is not a bad title to have." Then he took from his purse three golden sovereigns and handed them to me. "For the gelding, his saddle, and his bridle. I believe General Cromwell prides himself on paying for his horses. You can tell him that Colonel Mosley would not steal any that belong to him."

"The gelding was worth nothing, sir; and the saddle and bridle were well used," I said, prepared to return the coins to him.

"Then all the more pleased General Cromwell should be with the bargain." Wishing me good luck, with a nod of his head, Colonel Mosley dismissed me.

As I passed through the anteroom, I glanced at the lieutenant who was still waiting. He looked as comfortable as a sinner before the gates of heaven; and I was thankful that I was not Colonel Mosley's boy.

32
The Blacksmith

A wagon train moves as fast as the slowest team, and it may take three hours to cover the distance that a man on horseback can trot in one. A pace so slow was not to my stallion's taste, and at times I found him so difficult to control that I dismounted to walk. Faith, at such moments, would leap from the wagon in which she was riding and join me. Like a stray dog that had found a master and was afraid of being sent away, she would walk silently at my side. More than once her muteness enraged me, but when I turned to look at her, my anger would become shame.

On the second day of our journey, she suddenly asked, "They will hang him, won't they?"

I knew that "him" referred to her father. Rightly or wrongly, I answered, "Aye, it will be a miracle if he is saved."

"When they took him away, he asked to say good-bye to me; and I knew then that I would never see my father again. I cried . . . and cried . . . and then I prayed, but God did not hear me."

I said nothing but put my arm around her shoulders; then

like a stream running down a steep bed, she spoke about all that had happened to her. But there was no order to her tale; and in my mind I had to add time and place as she jumped from one incident to another.

As I suspected, she had been hidden in the Two Ravens. The morning after the arrest of Master Powers, his house-keeper had brought Faith to the almshouse; but she herself had quitted Oxford the same day. To this I made some bitter comment, but Faith seemed suprised. She did not feel that the housekeeper had deserted her.

Faith hardly spoke of Jack, whose only concern seemed to have been to keep her well hidden; and though this made me angry at my friend, it also pleased me. No harm had she fared at the inn, except that she had been left alone with her fears; and I could readily imagine the terror of those nights and days.

The act of finding words for her suffering seemed to lessen the pain. She even smiled once or twice, for in all hardship there is a point when something happens which will make you laugh later on. The very first night she had spent at the inn, Faith had imagined that a ghost had come to her room, but it had only been a cat. I told her how the same animal had frightened me on the stairs, and she laughed almost happily.

Yet what was I to do with her? Where could I take her once we reached Huntingdon, filled with soldiers as that town was? General Cromwell's family would probably take her in; but pride made me wish more for her than that she should become their scullery maid. More and more I became convinced that the right decision was to take her to the blacksmith and his wife, who had offered to give me a home, when they heard my father was going to take me "a-soldiering."

But I had not visited them, on my return from London, as I had promised myself I would. Debts which can only be repaid by gratitude are often the most difficult to redeem. A thousand excuses flew through my mind like so many black crows. In truth, most of the sins of youth are caused by thoughtlessness. The young are too busy tasting the world which is theirs to remember that it does not belong to them alone. I knew that both the blacksmith and his wife had kind hearts. "They are childless," I thought again and again; "they will not refuse to take Faith into their home." With the usual assurance of youth I decided that an "I'm sorry" would gain me entrance.

When I finally told Faith of my plan that she should stay with friends of mine who lived halfway between Cambridge and Huntingdon, she was not at all pleased. "I want to stay with you," she said. "I would not like to be among strangers."

"They are kind and good people," I argued, feeling hurt that she had not immediately submitted to my decision.

"I am sure they are." Faith looked thoughtfully down at her feet. The dress that Master Goodwyn had given her, though worn, was decent; and she had both shoes and stockings on. "But what if soldiers came? I used not to be afraid," she explained hesitatingly, "but now I am much afeared, especially at night."

"But in Huntingdon, you would often be alone in a town full of soldiers. I would be away most of the time . . . Besides, the blacksmith is much stronger than I am and his wife is the best woman I know." I told her how they had fed my father and me after my mother's death; and the thousand other acts of kindness they had done for us. I did not truly convince her; but finally she did yield and promised to stay, at least for the first few days, with my friends. Strangely enough, it was not all the praise I lavished on them that persuaded Faith, but my telling her that the blacksmith's wife had brought me into this world and that the hovel where I had spent my childhood was nearby.

We were well past Bedford when we bade good-bye to the driver of the wagon in which Faith had ridden. We were pleased to be alone. The weather had changed; winter was finally over. Some of the way we walked, I leading the stallion. But towards the end of our journey, we rode, Faith holding on tightly to my waist.

It was late afternoon when we arrived at the smithy. I helped Faith down and tied my mount to a ring on the wall. I could hear the blacksmith working at the forge. We stood in the doorway watching him until he noticed us.

At first he looked at me with a puzzled expression, then he grinned and said, "The pea is the same but methinks the pod is more splendid. You be welcome, Oliver, and so be your friend."

At the sound of the blacksmith's deep voice, Faith hid behind me, making my embarrassment even greater.

"I am sorry," I mumbled. "I am sorry that I have not come to see you before, but I have been . . ." And here I stopped, for I had been about to say "so busy"; but I realized that such a foolish lie might anger the blacksmith. "I am as grateful as a flea who gets drunk on your blood," I exclaimed instead, "and then does not return except when it is thirsty once more."

"Aye, my boy; but what would we do when we were at our leisure, if we did not have such bites to scratch?" We were still standing in the entrance and now the blacksmith caught sight of my horse. "And what do you call that great beast?"

I had called the stallion many endearing names, but had not thought of a proper one for him yet. The Irish Lord must have had a name for him, but I had never heard it. "Master!" I said suddenly and thought, "Yes, that is the right name for such a beast, for certainly he is a master among horses."

"Master," the blacksmith repeated and looked down at the horse's hoofs to make sure that he was well shod. "Water him at the trough. Then we will put him in the stable and give him some oats." While he spoke, the blacksmith smiled at Faith; but not once had she lifted her head so that he could see her face.

"And when will this war end and all of you make your peace with the King?" the blacksmith asked once we were seated at the table and I had told him of my adventures.

"Who knows?" I replied and shrugged my shoulders.

"There are those who say that it will not end until King Charles is truly beaten."

"Aye, that is men's talk." The blacksmith's wife looked angrily at both me and her husband, as if we were guilty of having started the war. "All they care for are their banners, their swords, and their great horses, and none of them thinks of what they trample down. They are all as vain as the cock in the henyard and about as useful."

"Aye, Mother, and that is woman's talk!" the blacksmith exclaimed and grinned.

"And what has the war ever done for that poor lass? Taken away her father and left no one to take care of her." The blacksmith's wife glowed with rage; and then suddenly she laughed, as if only at that instant she had realized that neither her husband nor I was a match for her.

"Oliver saved me," Faith said. "And he is very good; and it is not his fault there is a war."

"They are all peacocks, my girl." The blacksmith's wife looked affectionately at her husband. "And if they were not married to women with some sense, the world would have ended long ago." As she rose from the table, she patted Faith on the head. "Now you help me get the supper ready."

The blacksmith and I went out to close the smithy and sniff at the weather. "She is right," he began. "The high and mighty never ask what they trample down." He had picked up a hammer that lay on the anvil and tapped it gently against the iron. "Sometimes I think that if they left us alone, we would be better off. But they never will. The world is the anvil, and they are the hammer, and we are in between, getting all the blows."

I nodded, and then asked if Faith could stay with them for a while.

The blacksmith put down the hammer and looked around his forge. "If you had stayed with me, Oliver, I would have taught you how to master iron, and that takes skill and craft." Then he sighed. "We have never had a child to call our own . . . If Mother wants the lass, she can stay."

I thanked him, but he only growled in return. I knew what his words meant: he had offered me not only that I could stay, but that the smithy could be mine, as if I were his son. I felt ashamed because I didn't want to remain and become a blacksmith. He had offered me everything he had and I had ungratefully refused it . . . No, not ungratefully. As he closed the door to the forge, I said, "I am a peacock," and hung my head.

The blacksmith laughed. "Aye, Oliver, but would I not be the same, if I had young limbs like yours and a great horse to sit astride."

We both looked up at the sky to guess what the weather would be in the morning; then he put his arm around my shoulders and we walked into his house.

33

The End of My Journey

The blacksmith's wife was only too pleased to keep Faith in her home. There are those whose hearts have never known how to scheme. The rogues of this world — and they be the many — deem that these people have simple minds. This is not true; they have simple hearts. To comprehend the difference between sentimentality and sentiment is the very kernel of wisdom, the true center of any worthwhile tale told.

As I rode away the next morning, I had no such thoughts. I was pleased that all had gone according to my plans; and that the blacksmith and his wife had so readily agreed to play the parts which I had decided should be theirs. I had kissed Faith on the forehead, and for a moment she had clung to me; but I frowned and she let me go. This scowl of mine I regretted and tried to make amends for it by smiling and waving to her, as I trotted down the road.

I did not understand, then, what had happened to the little girl. I wanted her to forget all her unhappiness at my command, and be satisfied with whatever part of myself that I had the time or the inclination to give her. It was selfish of me, and I will make no excuses for it.

Spring was here, and the damp earth smelled of the coming of summer. I rode in a leisurely way. I passed several groups of soldiers but did not speak to them. I had decided to ride for Huntingdon, rather than Cambridge or Ely; though I did not know where I should find General Cromwell, I thought that Major Whalley probably would be there.

A few miles before the town, I let Master break into a gallop, keeping the reins tight so that his great neck was arched. "This may be the last time you ride him," I thought and sat even more straight in the saddle.

As I dismounted in front of the headquarters of the army in Huntingdon, I was dismayed to see several horses. A trooper came up to me and offered to hold mine. I gave him the reins and asked whether General Cromwell was within.

The soldier grinned and said, "He is with Colonel Ireton."

"Another promotion," I thought sourly, as I walked up the steps of the building. I told my name and errand to a lieutenant who was a stranger to me. There were many others waiting in the entrance hall. Some of them I knew; and several smiled and nodded to me.

More than an hour passed before the lieutenant finally indicated, by a wave of his hand in the direction of the General's room, that I might enter.

"So you are back." With these words Colonel Ireton

greeted me, and then added, "Flowers die but weeds thrive."

"Aye, sir," I said and bowed first to General Cromwell and then — not quite so deeply — to Colonel Ireton.

"We have a letter from Colonel Mosley in Aylesbury. It arrived this morning. In it he wrote of your adventures . . ." General Cromwell frowned to hide a smile.

"We did not send you to Oxford to save maidens in distress or to steal horses." Colonel Ireton was looking at me severely. "Obedience is the hub of the wheel."

"Aye, Colonel, but enterprise is the spokes." This time General Cromwell did smile, and my fears were over.

"Your dispatch from Oxford was not complete. You mentioned but a score of names." Colonel Ireton sniffed and turned his back on me.

"Aye, sir, I had not time for more. I concerned myself first with those members of the King's parliament who hailed from London, thinking that they were of most importance."

"You were pleased enough when you received it, Henry." General Cromwell looked with annoyance at his friend.

"Aye, they are traitors all. We need not have sent a boy to Oxford for that news." Suddenly the Colonel smiled, but his smile had no warmth. "And where is the maiden you have saved?" he asked.

"I left her with friends of my . . ." I stuttered and then said foolishly, "friends of my youth," which made both the Colonel and the General laugh.

"War ages a man quickly, Henry." General Cromwell

looked at me fondly. "And where is the horse you stole from Lord Inchiquin? I hope you haven't left that with friends of your youth as well."

"I have brought it for you, sir," I said proudly. "A finer horse there is not in all of England." Then I told of my meeting with the Irish nobleman and of how angry he had been because King Charles had not favored him but made someone else Lord President of Munster. All this interested General Cromwell and Colonel Ireton; and they asked many questions, most of which I could answer in a manner that pleased them. Nor did I forget to praise Master Drake.

When, finally, I had told my whole tale, General Cromwell demanded to see "his horse."

Master towered above the great crowd of soldiers who stood around him, eagerly commenting upon his strength and beauty. They made way for us, but did not go out of earshot, for the General was known to be a good judge of horses.

Carefully and knowingly, he looked at the great beast. At last, patting his rump, he turned to me. "I should have liked to see you galloping through Oxford on him," he said and glanced for a moment at Colonel Ireton.

The Colonel nodded, but I do not think that it was in agreement.

"He is jealous!" I thought with amazement. "He wants the General all to himself." And as we walked back to the house, I wondered if this could really be true. I was, after all, a mere boy of no importance.

As he stood on the threshold, General Cromwell's expression, which was usually grim, was as soft as when he spoke to his children.

"Henry," he said to the Colonel, "I have reached that age when my youth is more like a dream than a reality. I can recall its sweetness but know that it is past. The sun has climbed to its zenith and is now descending. The boy's name is Oliver; and I cannot say for sure that I would have acted as bravely as he has, but if I had, I would now be proud of it." The General looked at me and then once more at the horse. "I think my mare suits me best. I put you, Oliver, in charge of the stallion. We shall make use of both of you, be sure of that."

General Cromwell passed through the door, and as Colonel Ireton followed him in, he gave me a nod.

I ran down to my horse. Mumbling my thanks to the soldier, I grabbed the bridle, and swung myself into the saddle.

"You are mine," I whispered and clapped the stallion's neck. "Mine!"

I dug my heels into his flanks and let the horse gallop. Gone were all thoughts of what had happened to me. The stallion and I were one. And beneath us, under his thundering hoofs, was the earth; and for those moments that, too, like my great beast, was mine.

34
Epilogue: Boston, 1687

No story ever ends. It is the storyteller who grows tired. Like the mother who sits beside her child, singing it softly to sleep, he hums one last note and then gets up and walks from the room. I have more to tell of Oliver, but that will have to wait for another winter. For the present, let him gallop on his great horse, owning the whole wide world.

A month ago, the snow began to melt around the trees in my garden, and circles of green grass appeared. Spring is the most precious of the seasons, for its gentle rain stems from the fountain of youth and makes men into boys again. It is not only in the trees that the sap is rising when the sun returns to power.

On such a March day, when the sun was masquerading as if it were attending a May ball, I was talking to a neighbor. Here in the colonies, we have no other subject for conversation these days but Sir Edmund Andros, that tyrant whom King James the Second has made our master. My friend was mourning the loss of our charter. He said that we should have hidden it, and not let that brute of a Jack-in-office tear it into pieces as if it were a bill not to be paid.

I laughed then, but the following night I pondered over it. It might have been worth our while to have kept that document, Royal seals and all. Now it was lost, and for all I know, Andros might have used it to light his fire with.

But Connecticut still retains her charter, though those who know "sir tyrant" say it will not be for long. I have a friend in Hartford — a man who has courage to spare.

The very next day I borrowed a horse, for now I keep none of my own, and set out on a journey. My horse was not a stallion, nor did I gallop often. She was a gentle beast, a mare past her prime, whom life had taught that there are few things worth hurrying for.

My friend in Hartford thought my counsel wise; but he despaired, believing his fellow townsmen too timid for such an act. I hope that he is wrong and that they will manage to save their charter from Andros' claws. But whatever the outcome, I enjoyed my journey. It brought back sweet memories of all my rides in England, and the boy I once was.

When I arrived back in Boston from my mission and was dismounting by the stable, I could not help laughing out loud.

"You have kept faith with the boy," I mumbled to myself, as I took the saddle off the mare. "And what more or what better can an old man do?"